Larry Hansen Is Missing ...Maybe

Buddy Roy Baldry

ISBN: 978-1-989940-25-9
Copyright © 2021 Buddy Roy Baldry
Dimensionfold Publishing
Prince George BC CAN

Chapter 1: Bryce Springsteen

This is the type of guy Larry Hansen was. I mean, is. We do not want to jump to conclusions, but he has been gone for nearly two weeks. This is the type of guy Larry Hansen is. He is the type of guy who would point to your tie and say: "What's that spot on your tie?" And when you looked down at your own tie, he would sort of chuck you under the chin and you would have to laugh. Really, though, who does that and thinks it's funny? Maybe the first guy that thought up the joke in 1952 or something, but, come on. He enjoyed that sort of lame practical joke. Once he told me of his last job where he would take the top off a bottle of water and shove it upside down into a co-worker's pocket, so it leaked and made it look as though that person peed themselves. He never did that at my office, so I thought maybe he never did it at his last office either, it was just an idea for a joke that he never had the guts to carry out. That was the sort of joke that could get a person punched in the mouth.

He was not such a terrible person to be around, just the opposite. He was just the sort of guy to tell knock-knock jokes. And not ironically. Not the kind of knock-knock joke where you say, "the interrupting cow" and the recipient says, "the interrupting cow, who?" but before they can say that, you say "moooo" and interrupt the joke, making it funny or whatever. No, unfortunately his knock-knock jokes were of the "orange you glad you didn't say banana" variety. Just not funny. And he would for sure show you a ten-minute video on his phone of kids falling off a swing set or a cat compilation which you would feel obliged to say, "isn't that something" and stand uncomfortably watching the whole thing, trying to keep a smile going.

I am not doing a particularly good job describing why he was so unlikeable and likeable at the same time. I wish I could fully explain. He was just the type of guy you know would have been an annoying little fucker in high school.

I did not know him in high school, though. I met him in college. It's not as though Larry and I were close friends; we didn't even have the same circle of friends. I knew of him through his parties. He was not an athletic guy, mostly a nerd in disguise, so even back then I felt his parties were his attempt at a popularity I did not feel he deserved. Back then, I may have even been jealous. It would explain some things.

Maybe his peers did not care for Larry as much as they cared about his social gatherings. College kids love to party. His parties were always themed parties. Dress up as a super-hero, or a zombie, or a famous movie star, something dumb like that. Games as well: beer pong, beer racquetball, whatever game you could think of, Larry somehow involved beer. I grudgingly admit it was fun. I keep giving the impression that I do not like the guy at all, but that is not what I am trying to say. I don't dislike him. He was just always a bit over the top.

After college we did not keep in touch, not even on Facebook. It was not until twenty years later that he emailed me wondering about a position at the firm. I was surprised to hear from him at the very least, but also that he would be inquiring about a job. "I don't have much for you, Larry." I emailed after the usual patter of "wow it's been a long time, etc." And he emailed back immediately. He did not care that the position would only be data entry and not a very skilled job, or that the pay would not be that great. He had a good nest egg and was burned out of the life insurance game. He was leaving his position at Consumer Life. He wasn't quite ready to retire, of course, so a steady income at a low-pressure job would be fine.

Let me tell you, that was fine for me, as well. These entry level jobs attract younger people. Nothing against younger people, and I do not want to sound insensitive or risk a discrimination lawsuit, but let's be honest; the young women get pregnant and leave, or the job is just a springboard to something else. The young men were either too ambitious and you knew they would leave soon to find something more challenging, or they were slackers and would be perpetually late for work or not show up at all. It felt as though I was always training someone new. Someone of Larry's age and disposition sounded perfect.

Still, I want to have a happy office and I like to keep my people in the loop, so to speak, and I had a meeting with everyone to discuss it. No one seemed to care or pay attention and Larry started working for us. Same practical jokes, same positive and annoying attitude. He had a habit of calling everyone "good sir" whether it was a man or a woman. I considered this particularly annoying. As in, "good morning, good sir" or "how many copies of this would you need, good sir?" I hated it, but the others would chuckle, whether sincerely or not. I would try to feel the crowd out when he was not around by imitating his "good sir" to make fun of him, but no one took the bait. It was met with smiles. So perhaps I was the only one who was truly irritated. Which I could not understand. It sounds so stupid; "good sir" this and "good sir" that. Why be such a dork?

Ultimately all my staff liked him, and he fit in well. I tolerated him because he was honestly an all-right guy. He was always cheerful at work and never complained or gossiped. He did his job well; he was always twenty minutes early and always stayed late when he had to. I had no complaints. I gave him a raise within three months, which was early, but I felt no need to explain to anyone else that their raises would have to wait for next quarter. He was valued, if not essential. In truth, he was not really needed; a monkey could have done data entry. I suppose I did have a soft spot for him, after all. Plus, there were others much more high maintenance. Paul, for instance. Always moody, regularly late for work, always needing "to talk" with me privately. Pain in the ass. Larry Hansen, however, seemed to blend into the furniture. I was not sorry I hired him. He was good for office morale.

I keep saying "was" as if he is dead, or something. We don't know that he's dead. True, he has been gone a while and his wife has no idea where he is. The police did not take it seriously. Why? Because of that internet post and the newspaper article. Who reads a damn newspaper these days?

Here's the thing, the newspaper article and the internet post were reports on Larry Hansen's disappearance. Only, he hadn't disappeared. He showed the articles to his wife and I think he even called the newspaper to tell them there must have been some sort of mistake. He was not missing; he was right here. A typo? Of course. Unless there was another Larry Hansen, which was possible. It disturbed him enough to want to straighten it all out. I spoke to him earlier in the morning he actually went missing. He said he had a flat tire and would be late for work. It was lucky he had the spare tire. You should always keep a spare tire in your trunk.

It was strange because Larry's wife traced his credit cards and it showed he spent two nights in a hotel, but after that? Nothing. No more credit card use and he had not drawn any money from their accounts. It was not likely that a man such as Larry had a secret bank account and had been planning to leave. He just did not have that great an imagination. On the other hand, he and his wife were also childless, by choice I believe, so it was not unreasonable that he could just suddenly want to disappear; no children to think about how it would affect them. As well, his parents were deceased, so it is not far-fetched. But I have known him since college, and it does not seem in his nature. My staff saw him as happy and contented. He was not intelligent enough to be depressed and not too hurt by the world to want to destroy it. Just a guy who likes to play annoying practical jokes and thinks he is funny.

The point is, it was only a day or two after he vanished for real that we all became concerned. For anyone else, Paul for instance, we would say "oh, he is having one of his moods. He will text us all and fake quit again and come into the office looking for attention and edification that we appreciate him and then everything will be back to normal." Or Warren, for example, "well, he's off on another bender, he's missed Monday and Tuesday, leave him alone and he will sober up soon." So even though I let a lot of things slide around the office, Larry not showing up is something I took seriously. I am far too lenient on the rest of my staff. I think it's because of my name. Bryce Springsteen. I hate being called the boss, and I hate that my employees capitalize the word Boss in all their correspondence regarding me. I make every effort to be just one of the crew and not the Boss. What the actual fuck were my parents thinking? Therefore, when others took some unscheduled days off, I would not come down too hard on anyone. They would get a semi-stern lecture that would not amount to much in the long run.

With Larry, however, this was just not normal. And that is what Larry Hansen was: normal. Is. That IS what he IS: normal. Damn. He has been gone too long for Larry. Had he been kidnapped? Why would someone kidnap him? He is not rich enough for any sort of significant ransom. A sex slave? Laughable. Tall, skinny Larry with thin hair and a weak sort of chin that would make it difficult to fold towels or sheets. Mugged and murdered for a few dollars? Thrown in a river somewhere without a thought of who he was and what was left behind and no regard for human life whatever? That could be. But I am kidding myself when I say that there was no way he would disappear on his own accord. I honestly think he simply ran away, as unlikely as it was. Although it is disturbing that he has not used any credit cards or withdrawn any money. He ran away, I know it. And I think I had something to do with it. I am sleeping with his wife. I am sure he knows. No, I know he knows. His wife Marie told me he knows.

I swear it was an accident. Not an accident, in truth, but not on purpose, I mean, yes, on purpose, you cannot just have sex with someone and step back and say: "whoah, what just happened here?" It seems so dirty or sordid to say that I am sleeping with someone's wife, or that I am involved in an extramarital affair. It sounds sneaky and cruel. I am sure to someone on the outside looking in on the situation it would seem like all of that, but it did not feel like any of that. It was just something that happened. A few times. Eight times. But only on five occasions. It is over now that Larry has disappeared. Except for that last time (twice) since he disappeared, but it is truly over now. That last time was out of desperation, we were confused and worried and guilt ridden. We had wondered what he had done. So, to be certain of what we had done, we had to do it again. Twice. I am sorry for that last time, it was wrong. Both times were wrong that last time. The first time on that last time seemed wrong for obvious reasons, but also because it was a little rushed. The second time that last time seemed wrong for the right reasons. It was good, but wrong. Larry was missing, it was the last thing the two of us should be doing, we are not bad people. What if someone knew? Larry had been gone nearly two weeks.

I swear on my wife's grave, may she rest in peace, that I had nothing to do with Larry Hansen's disappearance. Other than making him want to disappear, of course, because he knew I was sleeping with his wife. My intention was never to make him want to disappear; it is not as though I wanted him out of the way so I could marry Marie. She was never going to leave Larry to be with me. She loved Larry, despite him being a pain in the ass and the sort of guy you knew would annoy the fuck out of you had you known him in high school. What happened between Marie and me was a mistake and would probably never happen again. I hope.

I met Marie only a few times over the last couple years and we never had a lot to say to one another. Just a nod and a hello at various company functions. There were certainly no sparks or fireworks between us. Not even close. It started during a game night at Larry's. I did not want to go. I always felt I needed to separate myself from my employees and not become too familiar. That weekend however, I was tired of being Bryce Springsteen, the Boss, I wanted to be just one of the crew, so I accepted his invitation.

What did I expect? He did not have a large house, but it was nice enough, with the basement decorated in what Larry called tasteful tastelessness. Duplicates of Van Gogh paintings were juxtaposed against framed photographs of Van Morrison. There was a pool table and a wet bar, Larry had not changed much since college, he certainly liked to entertain. That was the night I truly saw Larry Hansen's wife. She nodded and smiled as usual as she passed me a drink and the sparks or lightning did not come until much later in the evening, during the game of Charades. There were eight of us in four teams of two. Lisa from billing was on my team, which was a drag because she derided everything and thought everything was stupid. I agreed with her but at least I never said anything out loud. Paul and Warren were a team; bad pairing that one. Jeff and Jenny from accounting who we knew were related somehow but still wondered if they were a couple. And Larry and Marie.

We all wrote our clues on small slips of paper and folded them over to place them into Paul's Budweiser cap. Larry insisted he had a replica of a magician's hat somewhere, but we begged him to use Paul's cap, Lisa telling him to just get on with the fucking game. My clue for Lisa was the movie Top Gun which I described as, first word: a hand to my head, then a hand to my butt, and then a hand to my head again. I tapped my head until Lisa stopped saying, "Head, ass, head, ass ..." and began saying, "Can you do something else, Boss?" She was getting testy already and we had just started. So I countered with the second word: I pointed my finger and raised my thumb and pretended to shoot until she shouted: "Gun!" I nodded vigorously and went back to the first word of the clue. Instead of tapping my head this time, I simply raised my hand higher and higher in the air until she said: "Gun, gun ... high gun ... oh! Oh! Top Gun!"

Everyone cheered and Lisa high fived my genius Charade hands. Lisa lifted herself from the couch with a groan and adjusted her too tight blouse. She reached in the hat for her clue, and I sat in her place. She unfolded the paper and frowned as she read what was written. "Huh?" She squinted then looked up at the ceiling. She rolled her eyes and shook her head slightly, her massive earrings slapping her jowls. "Whose stupid ass clue is this?" She said to no one. She sighed dramatically and held up six fingers to indicate the number of words to solve. Many eyebrows raised.

"Six words," I said with anticipation.

"Yes, Bryce," Lisa winced at me, "six words." She sighed again and held one hand behind her back, and with the other hand began making a swinging downward motion, as if driving in nails with a hammer.

And I said, "Def Leppard's Rick Allen post 1985?"

Lisa stood with one arm raised and one arm still behind her back. She looked astonished. "Holy shit," She said, looking at the clue again. "That's right."

The room exploded with cheers. I glanced around, smiling. I was the man of the hour and I even astonished myself. It was one of those nights that would be talked about in the office for weeks and brought up again and again at other company functions and the Christmas party. I looked to Larry and he was giving me a thumbs up and squinting from grinning so hard. I grinned back and looked to his left at Marie. She was staring straight at me, not smiling. There was barely any expression, just a hard stare without blinking. I looked away quickly and I must have blushed. I felt the alcohol rise hot in my cheeks. When I looked back at Marie she stood and left the room.

I was sure I had done nothing to offend her at all since I arrived, and I was not sure why her reaction was in stark contrast to the others. I wasn't even sure what sort of reaction it was, and she was quiet the rest of the evening.

Call it cockiness at such a surprising victory on that one clue, but Lisa and I did not do well the rest of the game. I could feel her getting more and more annoyed with me as I tried to be overly clever with my Charades and answers, trying to recapture the glory. Despite our one dark horse winning round, we lost the game. Lisa was cranky and left before anyone else. Larry called a cab for me and I rode home in a tipsy, giddy silence.

Since my wife passed away four years ago, I made a habit of turning every light on in the house as soon as I got home, even if I was about to go to bed. For a year after Leigh died, I sat in the dark every night. Wake up, go to work, come home and stare at the walls until it was pitch black. It was killing me, and I needed to stop. That is why I did not find the folded note in my jacket pocket until my whole apartment was illuminated. On one side was a scribbled message: "So weird, this was my clue!" and a cell phone number. On the other side was the clue that Lisa had read: "Def Leppard's Rick Allen after 1985."

After a moment's consideration, I texted the number: "Not so weird, Def Leppard was my fave band when I was 12."

Immediately: bloop bloop: "OMG, me too!"

I texted: "ya I've seen them 3 times in concert." I added a musical note emoji.

Bloop bloop: "4"

I texted: "No way!"

Bloop bloop: "Yes! And once even before Rick Allen lost his arm! LOL."

I texted: "haha."

...

...

...

I stared at my screen. I watched the bubbles appear and then disappear. I did not know if I should wait or reply. I realized I was smiling, staring at an empty cell phone screen waiting for a message.

Bloop bloop: "This is Marie Hansen, btw."

I texted: "I know."

And that was how it started. Again, I am so reluctant to use the word affair because it did not feel like that. After thousands of texts and hours of phone calls, it felt as though we had known each other all our lives. It felt as if we had grown up together, like I knew her when we were twelve. We became good friends. Sure, we screwed when we met in person, but on the phone it was not like that at all. It was mostly about how our days went, how people were cruel to each other, did we think organized religion was ruining the world, how anti-vaxxers were nutjobs. It was not all sex sex sex. We rarely acknowledged the physical part; it was as if it never existed. We had found kindred spirits.

That night we texted for an hour. "Do you like Journey?" She bloop blooped.

I texted: "As in the band? Haha."

Bloop bloop: "duh! LOL."

I texted: "I love Journey. That album 'Escape' was a huge part of my childhood! The whole album."

Bloop bloop: "Ya!"

I texted: "For sure it was! Not just the one song they always play, but the whole album!"

Bloop bloop: "(smiley face emoji) Me too! 'Escape' was a huge thing for me."

Chapter 2: Paul

"Are you ever getting out?"

" ... "

What did she say?

And just like that: BAM. It hit him. Like a weight off his shoulders, or maybe like the final piece of a puzzle snapping into place. So simple. Because here behind the plastic shower curtain the hiss of the water was hypnotic, or something. Outside, it's all that. It's all that.

Are you ever getting out?

No.

"Paul?"

Shut up. "What?"

"I said are you ever getting out?" She asked again, "It's almost eight."

"I'm tired," Paul replied, but he does not think she heard him. She heard him; she just never *hears* him. That he is really tired, and not in a stayed up all night sort of tired. He means tired.

"I know you're tired, but it's almost eight."

Paul shaved and soaped up again, but he cannot put it off. And he does not want to get out. Once he gets out it all starts; comb your hair, brush your teeth, put on the deodorant, put the aftershave on, put the clothes on, the frigging tie. Then what? Breakfast. He will be late already with the traffic. Frigging work. He can't do it. Not today. He is tired.

Are you ever getting out?

No.

"I'm off," she said, and there was no sound but the shower. When Paul stood in the corner of the tub the water beat against the bottom. He calmed that noise by standing directly underneath the shower nozzle and then it was a soft sound as it poured off his body, gentle and reassuring. He swept it off his body and it fell in great slaps against the side of the tub.

Paul poked his head out from behind the shower curtain to see if she was really gone, because the sound of the water can play tricks on you. Make you hear someone that's not really there. His towel lay beside the tub. He should just shut the water off and get out, but damn ... he can't take it. He would like to crawl back into bed and pretend to be sick, but he had done that a lot in the last few months. It was just so warm in the shower right then, though. Warm and safe.

It was warm. He had to shut off some of the cold tap to make it warmer. The hot water was running out.

"Dad?"

Damn. That freaked him out. "What?"

"Are you getting out soon?"

"No."

"Come on, dad, I'm going to be late for school."

"Use the bathroom downstairs, Carla."

"It stinks."

"Carla, use the bathroom downstairs." And then she has gone because the door slammed, and she is swearing. He can hear her insolence going down the stairs.

The water was colder now. Does he have to get out? He shuffled his feet around the shallow water in the bottom of the tub and used his toe to play with the plug. It was the kind that cannot be removed, and he maneuvered it shut, the water started to fill the tub. He turned the cold tap nearly off and stood near the back to get out of the path of the steaming water. He shaved again. It felt like he had not used his razor in weeks. He thought about how time can get away from a person and suddenly it hurts to shave, there is so much growth.

The tub was full and he turned off the taps and sat in the water as Carla came back in the room. "I have to use the blow dryer," she said.

"Take it downstairs," Paul told her.

"And my makeup. Dad, I don't have time to be carting this stuff all around."

"Fine," he said, "use it in here."

"Well, are you getting out?"

"I'm not done my shower." He tried not to laugh but seemed unable to help himself. It was funny, wasn't it? He was never getting out of the bath.

"Dad?" She said, and Paul heard her coming closer to the tub. He covered his private parts just in case. "Are you crying?" she asked.

"No, I'm not crying," he said. "Why would I be crying?"

" ... "

"Why would I be crying, Carla?"

"I don't know," she answered quietly. "Are you going to get out?"

No.

"Just use the stuff here, Carla. I won't look if you don't."

"Gross," she said, and in ten minutes or so Paul assumed she was magically transformed. He splashed water around the tub. The sound it made was close to his ears and seemed intimate.

"Are you done?" he asked.

"Done."

"Can you make me some toast, then?"

"Dad?"

"Please, I'm hungry."

"Dad, why don't you get out and make it yourself?"

"I'm not done my bath."

"Dad, you're going to be late for work," she said.

"I'm not done my bath. Make me some toast, Carla," he said, mustering up all the mock authority he could handle. She left in a huff, but Paul heard her making toast downstairs in the kitchen. She's a good kid, really, he thought. And now he would have toast.

When she left Paul shouted to her to have a good day, but he did not think she heard him. He finished his toast and reached out to put the plate on the floor. He reclined in the tub. Maybe he should go to work. What would he say? It's hard to tell them, it's so difficult to explain. They don't listen, anyway. It's like everyone is too busy to hear you, or they are on their way somewhere too important for them to hear you when you tell them to have a good day.

If he got up ... if he got up ... if he got up and put on his clothes. He could start the car while the coffee was brewing. He had never heard the coffee splash that loud in the pot before. He got up and out ... and traffic was flowing slow. And horns honked a watery sound. And no one was at their desks when Paul got to the office. He panicked and realized he was so late that the meeting room was full, and they were all waiting for him.

"You've done it again, Paul," Bryce, the Boss said.

"What?" Paul asked.

"You've done it again, when are you going to stop doing it?"

"What?"

"Just tell me when."

What? What? What? Leave me alone, anyway, Paul thought. Fire me, I don't care.

"Are you home?" Bryce the Boss asked, and with one, old scaly looking hand picked up a phone that appeared at his side.

"Am I home?" Paul asked.

"I'm calling you," Bryce said. "Are you home?"

... The phone rang ...

"Are you home?" Bryce said again and Paul did not catch his meaning, they were standing right in front of one another. Then Bryce smiled and all his front teeth were missing, making Paul laugh. And then he understood; he was dreaming.

... The phone rang again ...

The water was cold, but Paul could not seem to move. He heard his heart beating like it was actually banging on the side of the tub.

Four more rings and the answering machine kicked in. "Paul, it's Jenny. It's nearly ten. Umm ... Bryce is looking for you and I told him you called in already. So, I hope you get this message so if you do show up I'm not caught in a lie. Umm ... I hope nothing serious is going on. Anyway, are you coming into work? Ok. Bye." Then

Jenny was gone, too. He felt guilty about not calling in, but then what would he say to them? Besides, there was no phone in the bathtub.

Paul drained some of the cold water out so he could fill the tub with hot again. He was getting all wrinkled and his hands were shriveled. He shivered until it was full. He knew he could not stay in the tub forever. That morning it had seemed like such a logical thing to do; just hide behind the shower curtain. Sort of like being dead without having to commit suicide. Of course, with suicide you would not have to try to explain to everyone what you were doing in the tub. And that you had no intentions of ever getting out. Ever. But suicide? He was not so sure about that.

He filled the tub three more times before his wife came home. It was lunch already? He should ask for more toast. He heard her clacking around downstairs in her high-heeled shoes. The sound softened when she entered the carpeted living room and then echoed and sharpened when she stepped into the kitchen. Then the sound stopped. It was sickeningly quiet, and he knew he was caught. It was so ridiculous, Paul tried not to laugh, but it was his laughter that ultimately gave him away. She was ascending the stairs.

"What are you doing?" she screeched, standing in the bathroom door. Paul let more water drain and turned the hot tap on, thinking it will act as a noise filter for when she really lays into him. He could not help himself; he began laughing harder.

"Paul?" Her voice was a little softer as she stepped into the room. He sensed that her hands were off her hips and she was debating whether to sit on the toilet seat or remain standing. "Are you crying?" She asked.

"I'm having a shower," Paul said.

"Why are you home from work?"

"I didn't go in. I'm having a shower."

"You didn't go in?" she asked, "What did you do? Are you sick? Why are you having another bath?"

"Not another one, the same one."

"Same one what?" She sat on the toilet seat.

"Same shower from this morning."

"Paul? I don't get it."

"What's not to get?" he said and then was suddenly tired of the game. "I couldn't get out."

"Of the house?" she asked. "What do you mean?"

"Of the shower," Paul said, "so I ran a bath so the water wouldn't run cold and I drain and fill it with hot water every half hour or so."

She sighed, "Paul, what are you doing?"

"I couldn't get out of the shower. I mean, I could have. I just didn't want to. No, that's not it. I couldn't get out of the shower, it seemed so nice in here. And I'm tired, you know what I mean?" he babbled, "What do you care?"

"What do I care?" she asked. She was crying. Or was it him? The shower curtain can do funny things to sound.

She left again and he heard her talking on the phone in their bedroom down the hall. "Is Darryl there, please?" Her voice was hollow.

Why would she be calling his brother?

"Darryl, it's me. I have a problem. Yes ... no, he didn't go in. Darryl, he's in the bath, he's been in there since morning. No ... in the bathtub ... since this morning."

And then her voice trailed off. She was either whispering or she had left the room.

He held his breath to see if he could hear what she was saying, but the drip from the tap had suddenly become so loud he could not even think. He put his foot under the tap to dampen the noise but all he heard was his own heartbeat in his ears and the soft trickling of the water as it shifted and conformed to his body. His wife walked in again.

"Darryl is coming over," she said flatly and took her place back on the toilet seat.

"What for?" Paul sneered.

"What do you mean what for? He wants to talk to you, that's what for."

" ... "

"I shut the water tank off," she said.

"You can't shut it off," Paul snickered. Or sighed.

"I turned the hot water all the way down. Or off. I don't know," she said. "Darryl told me what to do. All the hot water that's left in there is all that's left, so you may as well get out."

"I can't," Paul told her.

"Well, Darryl said he was calling Dr. Wanham and they're both coming."

"Dr. Wanker." Imagine that. In Paul's own bathroom. He could certainly think of two better people he would rather share his bathroom with. "I don't want to see him."

"Who? Dr. Wanham, or ..."

"Neither," he said and turned the water again. Damn. It was not as hot already.

"Paul, please don't cry," she said.

"What are you talking about?" he asked her. She was going hysterical, he thought. "I'm not crying. Turn the hot water back on, I'm just going to soak another ten minutes or so and then I'll get out."

"Really?"

"No." It was the truth. She deserved more than lies, he supposed.

"Just talk to Dr. Wanham," she said, "and maybe you can go to his office again. Things were nicer then, no?"

" ... "

"I can't live like this anymore," she said, and then Paul heard a car pull into their drive. His wife got up and left without saying anything. They were here. And who knows who they've brought this time. Probably cops if history teaches us anything. Damn. You see? It does not matter where you are, they find a way to come and get you. It's like they can see right inside your mind or something. No, not as science fiction as all that, but something. You have to be careful what you say, or they will use it against you. He can hear them in the kitchen, talking low. Laughing their asses off, more likely. It was pretty funny, when Paul considered it.

"Paul?" His brother, climbing the stairs. "You all right?"

Paul laughed. Or sobbed. "Sure," he said. It was nice in here, too. He knew they would take him out of the bath no matter what. He could kick and scream and fight, but either way they would get him out. He may as well just get out on his own. Fine, Paul thought, I'll get out. But I'm not getting dressed.

Chapter 3: Warren

Warren could care less that Larry Hansen has been AWOL for two weeks. He never really knew the guy in the first place. When Larry would approach him, Warren would walk away, that is how much he knew of the guy. Annoying as fuck. Especially in the morning. Who the hell is that cheerful in the morning? No one needs to talk to each other in the morning. Just get your own coffee, get to your workspace, and shut up. Maybe around ten AM people can start talking to each other. But first thing? Piss off. Before ten Warren just needs to slip into the washroom, lock the door, and take a swallow of spiced rum. Then.... Then everyone can talk about their weekends. Warren will even contribute with some made up activities: "I saw a great movie" or "Went out to the lake with some relatives" just to get his co-workers off his back. Truth was, most of his weekends were spent drunk, watching Netflix or YouTube, and arguing with idiots on Facebook and Twitter. It would start Friday night right after his shift ended. He did not mind going to work; it was the waiting around eight hours to go home he hated. Once home there would be oblivion. Besides, selling pills was easier and nearly paid the same.

He never understood the druggies he sold to. Why would you want to take something that made you think more, dance more, or stay awake longer? There was only one reason Warren drank, that was to black out and pass out. Escape. Escape from what? Maybe that he was thirty and lived with his grandmother. That he has not had a real girlfriend in a few years. That he sells pills to idiots to supplement his shitty income at a shitty job that he could not give a shit about. That he has not paid a single bill in four months, including the people that supply him the pills that he is supposed to sell on their behalf.

"Warren?"

What?

"Warren?" His grandmother's voice, far away. She must be upstairs looking for him in his room. *Close this window. Hide the bottle. And quick, close this window.*

"Warren? Where are you honey?"

Close the damn window. Every time he clicked the X, another window opened, the blue bar at the bottom of the screen filling up telling him there were more images to download. He did not want pictures to download. He wanted the pictures gone. He wanted to close the window. He could not be putting all this stuff on his grandmother's ancient computer.

"Are you down there, Warren?" She was at the top of the basement stairs. She knew he was there; she must be able to see the light was on. "Are you on the computer?"

"I'll be up in a second, gramma," he shouted. X. Another window opened. X. Another window. Come on, come on. Wait? What site was that? No time to mark it, just close the window.

"Are you on the internet, Jeremy?" He heard her coming down the steps. One. Two. Getting faster with confidence. Why couldn't he just watch porn on his phone like everyone else. Always on this archaic computer in the basement, but it was easier to hide his bottles down here. Oh shit, the bottle. He took it from the desk and put it underneath and back toward the wall. It tripped up over the wires there and spilled. Dammit.

"Jeremy?"

"What? What is it gramma? It's Warren." He swiveled in the chair to face her.

"What are you looking at here?" Her head bobbed like a boxer, trying to see the computer screen behind him.

"It's for work. See?" He moved back. Please please please.

"Chesterfields?"

What site is that? "Well, sure. It's a thing we do."

"Is that E-Bow?"

"E-Bay."

"A-Bay?"

"E-Bay, gramma. No, it's not." He disconnected. "I just might have hit the wrong thing there."

"Those computers." She turned and waved her hand in the air, dismissing Micorsoft and everyone like them. "I need your help, Jeremy."

"Sure, gramma." He followed her up the stairs, stopping every third step to let her get a head start. "What do you need?"

"Sugar is up in the tree."

"She won't come down?"

"She is very high, I don't know how on earth she got up there, but she won't come down." His grandmother stopped at the top of the stairs and looked both directions. The living room to the left, with dusty couches where no one sat, and the stairs leading up to their rooms. The kitchen to the right and the backdoor leading out onto the deck.

"Sugar? Gramma?" He touched the back of her dress, bulky gramma underneath.

She shook her head slightly, "Of course." Moving again. Through the kitchen and out to the back yard. "I don't know how she got up there. If you can't get to her, what do we do? Do we call the fire department?"

"Do they still do that sort of thing?" Warren asked her.

"Did they ever?" She turned and looked at him. Frowning. "Jeremy?"

"It's Warren," he said.

"Oh." She looked disappointed. "I'm sorry, Warren." She was holding the screen door open with one spotted hand, blue veins like a road map ran its length. "I don't know how she got up there. If you can't get her ..."

"Sugar?" He called, and nudged his grandmother gently forward, letting the screen door slam shut behind them. Paint from the deck peeled away and stuck to the bottom of his bare feet. It was moist out here, the summer heat already gone. Warren scanned the back yard. The grass needed mowing and the hedges were grown over and wild looking. Two birch trees stood like soldiers in either corner, only a few feet from the sagging fence. "Which tree? I can't see her."

"Not those," his grandmother said, one crooked finger accusing the large oak tree in the middle. "That one, there. Do you see her?"

"That one?" Warren asked. "How would she get up that one?" He was looking at the trunk. Scaly and dead, it did not branch off until ten or fifteen feet in the air. Then its branches were hostile and brittle. Birds avoided it.

"Do you see her?" his grandmother asked.

"No," Warren said, his eyes climbing the tree. Nothing there. Not even leaves clung to the old thing anymore. He picked off each skeletal branch one by one, its fingers reaching up to the sky for forgiveness at being a tree which would never bear fruit, a tree that had no...

...there...

But not like he thought. Sugar was not clinging to a branch, mewing and searching for rescue. Not clawing at the branches for a foothold. Not being very cat-like at all. Sugar was hanging by her neck from a noose. A small noose fashioned especially for her. About twenty feet up one of the stronger branches. Her frail body swayed with the wind, back and forth and around in circles. Her tiny paws stretched or curled as if begging like a dog for her life. All that was missing was a small kitten hood. It was a cruel execution.

"Do you see her?"

"I see her," he said, the spit clicking and drying in his throat.

"How do you suppose she got up there?" his grandmother asked.

"I don't know," Warren lied.

"Sugar!" She clapped her old hands together. The sound was like one of those branches from the oak snapping and falling to the ground. "Sugar, you come down here this instant. Bad kitty!"

Dead kitty, Warren thought. All nine lives, just like that. "You go inside, gramma. I'll get her down."

"Don't you hurt her, Jeremy."

"Warren, gramma," he said.

"Don't be ridiculous, he is too small to do something like that to Sugar."

"No, gramma, I'm Warren."

"Although that young rascal does have a mischievous streak in him, like his mother." She shuffled her feet as Warren moved her inside, flakes of paint following her and resting on the kitchen floor. He sat her in a chair facing the inside of the house. "Are you making tea?" she asked him.

"Tea?" He paused by the door, his hand along the doorjamb. It complained under his weight. "You want tea, gramma?"

"Tea? Yes, please, Jeremy. That would hit the spot."

He upset the pots and pans in the cupboard reaching for the kettle, they fell to the floor and he swore. He glanced over but his grandmother had not heard. He rearranged the small cupboard and found the kettle and filled it with hot water. Would that make it boil faster? Or perc? Or whatever. So. Cat now, or cat later? Could he even get the thing down? And when he did get it down, then what?

There was a shrill whistle. The tea. "Gramma?" He set the cup on the table in front of her. She was slumped to one side, breathing through her mouth. Sleeping? He could hear the mucus in the back of her throat. "Your tea is here, gramma."

"Fuck off." Barely audible. Still, no mistaking what she said.

"Fine." He whispered.

The cat looked further up than before. When he was on the deck of the house, he only had to look up ten or fifteen feet, maybe a little more. Now, he could make out the cat swaying in the breeze, but he could not make out a way to get up there to get the dead thing down. He should call the fire department. If they still did that sort of thing, if they ever did that sort of thing. Would they call the police? Something like a cat hanging from a noose in a tree could not just be ignored. They would definitely contact someone Warren would not want contacted. There was no question; he would have to get the stupid cat down by himself.

It wouldn't be so bad. He climbed trees all the time when he was a kid. Even in this very yard. Although he did not remember trying to climb this particular tree. And not half drunk. Its trunk was as wide and scaled as an elephant's foot. He ran his fingers along the bark. Deep groves. Spiders escaping. No footholds. He walked around its base, stepping over exposed roots. There was no way without a ladder. Sugar's kitty corpse was swaying harder, calling him to hurry.

He found the ladder in the garage. It was old and the third rung was missing, or the twentieth, depending on which way he held it. It was hard to find a level place at the bottom of the tree, and even more difficult as he began to climb. The ladder moved a good two inches when he was a third of the way up and felt like it kept shifting with each step. He stopped and held his breath. There was a sharp ping in his stomach that went all the way through his groin. When it went away, he took another step. Each rung groaned and threatened to break. Halfway up, now, and he still could not reach the cat. Don't look down, don't look down. He looked down. Damn. He was higher than he thought. How on earth did someone...

He would need a branch. The old tree reached one of its appendages out to him and he snapped it off with one hand while clinging to the ladder with the other.

Another step. He reached out and up with the branch. There, he could just reach the tip of Sugar's hanging claw. One more step. He heard a sharp crack and he went still. Please don't let me fall, please don't let me fall, he whispered. Another step.

As if it were a piñata, he began belting at the hanging cat. Would the small noose give way? The cat swung out and back, and he struck it again. Out and back, closer this time. Another whack with the branch and on the fourth attempt he was able to reach out and catch Sugar by her fur. He gagged as he held the dead cat. "Ok, then." He moaned, one hand holding the cat, one hand holding the ladder rung. "What now?"

Reluctantly, he let go of the ladder and reached up to get hold of the miniature noose. The ladder slipped to the left. "No, no, no, no..." He held the noose with both hands and gave a slight tug. He felt his toes curling as if that would clutch the ladder more tightly. He could feel the rope give a little. One more tug and it would break. One more pull.

The ladder slipped again. One of Warren's legs stayed on the rungs, the other lost its grip and clawed at the rough bark of the tree, struggling to find a foothold. "Come on, you dirty..." Tug. " ...son of a ..." Tug.

The ladder slipped away entirely and sank slowly down the length of the tree. Warren was grasping the rope and the dead cat. He was losing his grip as he felt Sugar's body compressing under his weight.

Success. The rope broke.

"Water?" But the nurse walked past, brushing against the open curtain that was meant to give him privacy. It billowed out and settled. "Could I get some water?" he said louder. "Please?" Someone would hear. Come on, pills, kick in.

"Is this Warren?" The curtain drew back with a shriek. A nurse with a bulging white uniform held out a small paper cup. "Water?" she offered. Warren took the cup in both shaking hands.

"Can I get something for the pain?" He implored, pointing to his leg. He drank the water in one gulp.

"I can get you something, yes." She took the empty cup from his folded hands. "Let me just ask the doctor first."

"Where is the doctor? He hasn't come around yet, I've been waiting..."

"Everyone is waiting. He'll be here soon," the nurse said.

"And something for the pain?"

"Right away." She smiled and turned to leave.

"Right away?"

"That's what I said." He heard her sing song as she walked away.

He called after her, "But if you have to see the doctor first to get the pills, how can you do that right away?" She stopped and faced him, smiling and blinking. "I mean, if he's so busy, and all that?"

She wagged a finger at him and winked. "Be good," she said and then she was gone.

The pain was eating and tearing at his leg. It was angry, pulsing and throbbing. Stupid cat. His fingers fumbled at the breast pocket for the note inside. For some reason the police came before the ambulance did, half an hour after he fell. He took the note that was tied around the cat's neck before he passed out. Should he eat the note before someone found it? But who would find it? They were not going to frisk him. He fell out of a tree and broke his leg, he was not caught stealing or anything, he was a victim here. No one would care about a note. It was meant for him and not his grandmother, anyway. The note read: "The $2500 you owe. Thursday. Next time not the cat. Next time we break your leg."

Funny

And it was $2000. Maybe they were charging him interest. But $500 interest? Drug dealers should stick to drugs, Warren thought, because they can't do math.

"This is Warren?" Like magic the doctor appeared from behind the curtain, shielding a clipboard from Warren's view. "I have the x-rays here, your leg is indeed broken."

"I could have told you that." Warren said.

"Yes, well. We'll set the cast and then..."

"How long?"

"Pardon?"

The cast, is that on a long time? Or is it like, how long does it take, to like, heal..."

"We leave it on for six weeks and then see..."

"...six weeks..."

"...how it does after that." The doctor paused as if trying to decide something. He pulled up the chair next to the bed and sat down, removing his glasses, he looked at Warren until Warren had to blink and lower his eyes. "I want to talk to you about your grandmother," the doctor said.

"Six weeks." Warren groaned. "Wait. What? What happened to gramma?" He tried to sit up and the doctor put a firm but gentle hand on his shoulder and held him to the bed,

"I was speaking with your grandmother," he continued, "She keeps calling you Jeremy. Is Warren your middle name?"

Warren relaxed. "Jeremy is my dad."

"Yes, well. Your grandmother insists on calling you Jeremy. So, I spoke with her for quite some time." He cleared his throat and patted the curtain with his fist. It responded softly and kept coming back for more. "She's an interesting lady, isn't she?"

"Yes, she is," Warren said, "I have a job, how can I go to work with a cast on?"

The doctor gave a small shrug as if the question did not matter much. "How long have you been staying with you grandmother?"

"Six months?" Warren offered.

"Six months." The doctor frowned slightly. He punched at the curtain again. He looked to Warren like he was deep in thought. "Have you noticed anything peculiar about your grandmother, lately?"

Not really, Warren wanted to say, I drink a lot. "Peculiar?" he said instead. "You met her, you tell me." He tried to smile and was met with another frown.

"Yes, I see," the doctor said. "Have you noticed anything different about her behavior?"

I am really drunk most of the time, Warren wanted to say. "Like?"

"Well, for example, her calling you Jeremy, that's a little different, don't you think?" The doctor used the clipboard and traced an imaginary line along the curtain, watching it expand and deflate. He is trying to get to some sort of point, Warren thought.

"Sure, but she's old," Warren said, holding his hands out and trying to shrug. Everything hurt. "Right?"

"Has she forgotten anything else?" The doctor turned back to Warren.

"…"

"The year, for example. Has she ever forgotten the date?"

"Well, everybody..."

"No, I mean drastically. You have been at her home six months, you say? Your grandfather is no longer with us, correct?" Warren nodded. "Has she ever called you by her husband's name?"

"That's sick, man. Come on." Warren tried to shift away from the doctor and his leg screamed at him to stop. He obeyed.

"She saw her cat hanging from that tree, didn't she?"

"I think so," Warren said. "Unless she's blind, too." He tried a laugh. No smile from the doctor. "That was just a joke," Warren said, feebly.

The doctor put his glass back on his face and scanned the clipboard in his hand. "She saw it hanging there, right? Not in the tree, but hanging from it?" He pulled his glasses off again and squinted down at Warren. There was a red mark on his pasty face where the nosepiece was. "Hanging from a noose, is that right?"

"She must have." He did not like where this was going. "That was something between me and some people. It has nothing to do with gramma."

"Hmmm..."

"What?"

"What?" The doctor lay the clipboard across his lap and folded his hands over it.

"What, hmmm...," Warren said, irritated. "What was all that about?"

"The cat is neither here nor there," the doctor said suddenly, his mind made up about something. "I have a feeling about your grandmother. I think she is suffering from Alzheimer's. This is a disease that..."

"I know what it is." Warren waved his arm in the air, hoping to propel the conversation forward and away from the hanging cat. "She's senile."

"Well, that's not necessarily..."

"But Alzheimer's? She's pretty much done for, right?"

"Well, no." The doctor gave a patient smile. A patient smile used on patients. "It's a little complicated without doing some formal tests, and still there would be no conclusive evidence that could suggest the disease. After an autopsy, sure, but while the patient is still alive, I'm afraid it's only guesswork."

They have completely forgotten that I am lying here with a broken leg, Warren thought. All because of my grandmother in the first place. Stupid cat. Stupid drug dealers. "So, what's the bottom line here, doctor..." Warren looked at the man's shirt for a nametag. There was none. "Doctor?"

"Well, the thing is, with your leg, my concern is for your grandmother." The doctor tapped Warren's toes lightly with the edge of the clipboard. Warren winced.

"My leg is broke and you're worried about my gramma?" Warren said. "I don't get it."

"How would she get along, is what I mean." The doctor continued. "Would she be all right if you were incapacitated? Let's face reality, you are incapacitated."

"Five weeks, right?"

"More like six." The doctor eyed Warren as though he were trying to reduce the healing process by some trick. "I am sure you will be able to go to work very soon, but what I worry about is your grandmother. I don't think the two of you would be good for each other in her house. Is it a large home?" Warren shrugged. "I don't know if it is a good idea..."

"So, you suggest," Warren held his arms wide, waiting to receive whatever solution was offered. "What?"

"She should be in a home." And there it was. Frank and to the point. The doctor put his gold wire rimmed glasses on and lowered his chin, eyeing Warren over the lenses. "But I am not familiar with your situation," he said. "Is there someone... is there anyone you can call?"

Warren thought. He watched the light gleam off the doctor's forehead. It seemed slippery, as though what little hair was left would slide right off. It reminded him of someone, and he felt a chill. "I suppose I could call..." He rubbed his temples. "I guess I could call my dad." He said it quickly, as if spitting the words out of his mouth. He watched the doctor's satisfied face. The pain in his leg was suddenly very small.

Chapter 4: Lisa

There was a song coming from the small overhead speakers that Lisa could not place. The tune stuck in her mind and she was having trouble concentrating. It was an early 80's song, not quite a hit, but what was called new wave or post punk back then. She only recognized the melody because her sister played it incessantly while they would get ready for school in the mornings. All those years ago when she and her sister were so young. And so much skinnier. And still speaking to each other. Canned drums with soft horns doing the vocal part for a song that was once considered cutting edge, or rebellious. Now coming from a tiny speaker in the ceiling of a department store.

Why did all these stores have the same strange music coming from the roof? Why did they all carry the same stark lighting? The same smell? When they were in the city, she and her husband ate in the fanciest of places. Places with coat checks and valets even. They went to fine shopping centres, not malls. Centres where they would wrap your purchases and carry them out to your car. And the hotels? The rooms were so large, with two separate bathrooms. Larger than their first house, probably. The hotels would pick them up from the airport in limos. She was a mayor's wife, after all. Theirs was not the largest city in the country, but certainly large enough that she should be treated with come sort of nobility or reverence. It made her feel like the queen she was supposed to feel like. A thousand miles literally and figuratively from that small northern town where she grew up.

Coming home was always a disappointment. The malls here were small and second rate compared to the ones they went to across the border. Here they were filled with teenaged girls and the middle-aged useless men who came to ogle them. And as far as the eye could see, obesity. Her included, she thought sadly. Still, they would all gather in the food court and devour the grease and calories and gluten. Coming home from the cities down south always reminded her she had escaped from one uninspiring small town to another. Eventually all the towns would seem small to her. No, she would insist to her husband, she was not depressed. How to explain? She was just bored. Anything new and exciting would lose its sheen over time and start to dull at the edges. Like a song that was once so badass but now could be heard as muzak through a small speaker in the ceiling.

Her husband implored her to get out of the house and get into the world. Sometimes there were days, weeks even where she did not have contact with another person. She had no friends, and she did not care. The wives and husbands of the other city employees did not interest her. She tried all the fundraisings and causes and diets and petitions. Kiss my ass, Lisa thought. Boring. She needed something.

She left the houseware department of the store and stepped thoughtfully through lingerie. The woman pinning up undergarments to a grid rack smiled at her. Recognized her, of course. They all recognized her, but they never quite seemed to know from where. Her husband was a different story. When they went out, he got a lot of attention and, by association, so did she. If he were here with her in the lingerie section the woman working there would have said, "Oh, hello Mr. Mayor. Mrs. Mayor." Or would she have? Actually, no one had ever said hello Mr. and Mrs. Mayor. It was implied, though. When she was out alone, a faint smile of recognition was all she got.

She fingered a black bra with frilly things up the side where her boobs would hang out. Would William be interested? That was laughable, but maybe. She held it up for the salesclerk to inspect. "Very nice?" her eyes asked. The girl smiled back. There were no wrinkles around her eyes, she was too young to be interested in anyone or anything. The clerk quickly turned her back on any impending conversation.

Oops... into the purse...

Lisa had thought about having an affair around a year ago. Something to spice things up. Something to give her a thrill and shake up her world. Her world was a green and shallow pond. She wanted something to stir it all up and get the minerals and dirt swirling to the surface again. Something to muddy up her waters, so to speak. But how does one go about having an affair? And with whom? She was not likely to go on-line to one of those sordid sites with all those creeps. Who knows who they were or what they would do? Besides, eventually they would find out who she was. Who would want to sleep with the mayor's wife? More importantly, why? They would try to extort money from her. What an embarrassment for her and William. He did not need that sort of scandal with his latest approval ratings. He was not faring well.

The affair was a fleeting and stupid idea after all. She did not enjoy the flirting that would have to precipitate an affair. Most men were stupid when it came to flirting. They either advance with no solicitation whatsoever, no indication that the recipient was interested. They would come on heavy when faced with indifference or even outright hostility. On the other end of the spectrum, there were men who would not know you were flirting with them if you lifted your blouse and rubbed the glasses right off their face with your tits. There was no in-between.

Really, why have an affair? It was not like she needed sex. She and William had unremarkable and unnecessary sex once a year at best. Usually after too many drinks at some tedious party. She did not desire it, nor feel like she was missing out. She was just a few years short of caring. To be fair, even as a young woman sex was not something she was concerned with. Even in her prime she couldn't care less. It was messy. She never orgasmed during intercourse, and even when she climaxed alone with a toy she would think, this is what all the fuss is about? No. Not interested in an affair.

"Are these on sale this week at all?" Lisa held up a pair of yellow panties with inlays. She waited until the young clerk turned around, so her name tag showed. "Debbie?"

"No, I don't believe so," Debbie said curtly.

"Lisa," Lisa said.

"Pardon?" The salesclerk turned only slightly toward her again.

"My name is Lisa," she said hopefully. "Lisa King."

"Then I don't believe those are on sale this week," the clerk said, "Lisa."

"Thank you," Lisa said, and the young woman turned her attention to something else. Oops... into the purse...

Then, for a time, Lisa decided perhaps she could become an alcoholic. She had seen a documentary on addiction, and while she had empathy for the people and families who were afflicted, one theme kept cropping up and worming into her conscience. Blackout. Oblivion. Escape. So interesting. It sounded like exactly what she needed. She would not do it like that juvenile Warren, though. She could hide it better than that.

She was never a big drinker. Not in high school, not in college, not in her twenties when she and William were just starting out. Even later at the meet and greets that were integral to her husband's career, she preferred sparkling water over sparkling wine. It was the taste that turned her off. And beer? Forget it.

She tried her experiment when she knew William would be out of town for a few days. She started with wine and that lasted the weekend. On Friday she went to winery and toured the facilities and was bored. She had some dull conversations with some other women her age and bought three bottles of a dark red they told her would go fine with the steak and shrimp for the party she was having. There was no party. Maybe a party for one. That got a rare smile to herself on the drive home.

That first night was fine. There was a glow and a buzz that was unexpectedly nice. She watched a few movies that she could not remember the next day and end even reached out to some college friends on social media. She went to bed fully clothed. In the morning, or more precisely at 11:30, she woke with the worst pounding in her head she had ever felt. It dawned on her that this was not the answer. It was a worse idea than the affair. She glanced at her phone and saw three messages from people she had contacted the night before and whom she had no interest in ever speaking to again. What had she been thinking? "Wow! So nice to hear from you! It's been years!" Delete. Another read: "So, you finally decided to apologize?" Delete. She deleted the third without reading.

It may have been the worst feeling, but she knew a one-night experiment did not make a conclusion. Didn't alkies drink in the morning? The thought made her gag as went to the liquor store in the nearest strip mall to buy whatever wine had the most appealing label. She did not know wine. The second night was nowhere near as pleasant as the night before. This was a night of stumbling and falling and throwing up and passing out on the bathroom floor.

Still, like it was some sort of duty, she visited the liquor store the next day. No makeup, hair not done, in her slippers and sweatpants. Wow, she thought, this happens fast. How quickly we degrade. She was aware that this was not going to work; it was only the third day and being an alcoholic was more boring than she could have imagined. She stood with her bottles in a lineup that seemed exceptionally long. There were seven people ahead of her. Her brain was aching, her boobs were sweating, and she sensed that she smelled awful. Would people recognize her? Of course someone would recognize her. What had she been thinking? This was an absolute mistake and she had to get out of there as quickly as possible. She was not a drunk, she was just bored.

She turned away from the lineup with the full intent of replacing the bottles on the shelves and going home, cleaning up the mess she left, and just going to sleep. As she shouldered past the other shoppers, whom she now judged as total lushes and helpless drunks, she felt awkward holding the three bottles and her large purse. Wouldn't that just be typical if she were to drop the bottles and have them smash on the floor, creating a scene? So, just for safety and convenience, she slipped the bottles in her purse ...oops... and walked through the aisles. Yet, when she got to the shelf space the bottles had been, she just kept walking. She could not explain it to herself even afterward. She could hear the bottles clinking softly together in her purse as she walked out the sliding glass doors. There was no alarm, and no one was chasing after her. She sat in her SUV with her purse and the bottles in the seat next to her. She could see in through the liquor store windows. Everyone was going about their business, people shopping, cashiers ringing items through, men stocking shelves. No one had even a clue that she had walked out with three bottles of wine that, even to her, seemed expensive. No one knew but her. At that moment she felt a tingling sensation she had not felt in... well, had she ever felt it? She sat in the SUV in the liquor store parking lot and slid one hand between her legs.

Whatever song was playing on those ceiling mounted speakers had ended and Lisa King folded her purse under her arm and left the lingerie section. She listened to her shoes clack on the tile. Men's wear. Boy's wear. There was a small boy's T-shirt sporting some sort of cartoon character, she was not sure ...oops, into the purse... which one it was.

The overhead speakers blocked out the music momentarily: "29 to Boy's Wear. 29 to Boy's wear." The announcement fizzled and cut out and the music resumed. Was she caught? Should she put it back? She shuffled a few feet over. It was time to leave. But there was still the perfume to look at, it's what she came for, after all. She stepped into a main artery aisle. There were shelves of towels on sale, bright green ones with orange stripes. Hideous. She opened her purse.

"Is there anything I can help you with today?" There was Debbie, holding one of the towels and refolding it, looking at Lisa suspiciously.

"I think I'm fine," Lisa said, "but can you tell me where the perfume is located?"

"I'll take you," Debbie said. The young clerk did not look behind her as Lisa followed. Lisa let her hand slide down the towels and onto the smaller hand towels. So rough. So very useless in her own home... oops...

It felt like ages ago since she left that liquor store parking lot that fateful day, but her elation was short lived; William was home early from his trip and was there when she pulled into their drive. He was furious, as he should be. The broken glass on the coffee table, the piled-up dishes in the sink, the puke on the carpet, the eight empty wine bottles on the kitchen counter already gathering flies around their necks. "What in the actual fuck?" was what he actually said. But he soon became cautious and tender and suggested rehab. She explained everything. She was just so bored; she did not want to be an alcoholic. She even admitted to considering an affair to which he was more understanding than she wanted him to be. "I know what you need, right now," he told her, "We are going to

get you some therapy, but first, you are going to get a job."
He held up his hand when she began to protest. "Just for a
month or two to keep you occupied, then we will figure
something out. I have a friend that will make a position for
you in his firm. Bryce is a good man, and he will get you
something. We will figure this out." Then he held her, and
she allowed him to make love to her that night in a messy
and uninspired way. She even slept well. Not because of
the lovemaking, not because of his tender offer to help her
through whatever she was going through. It was the
thought of walking out that door with the liquor bottles in
her purse while no one even had a clue.

And now, standing in front of the mid-priced
perfume in a low-level department store, she still felt some
of that. But the quota was filled. When the risk and the
thrill started to ebb, she knew it was just time to go home.
Anything more would cheapen and lessen the experience.
Just once more. As she ... oopsed... a few bottles of
perfume in her purse, bottles she knew would be thrown in
a dumpster later, she glanced up and into the eyes of a man
she knew. He was watching her.

There was no mistaking or denying what was
happening. He had seen her put the bottles of perfume in
her purse. There was no pretending they did not know
each other. He was staring right at her. His face flushed
and he turned quickly and walked away. She tried to
follow him, but it was as though he had vanished. He saw
her do it. He knew she did it. And she knew that he knew
she did it. This was not good.

What the hell was he doing here?

Chapter 5: Paul

Paul's brother called him early in the afternoon and voluntold him that he was picking him up and they were both going to do a bit of mild manual labour. "This will do you a world of good, buddy boy," he told Paul. Bad timing, but how could Paul say no? After all his brother had done for him; stood by his side throughout all of Paul's bullshit. He did tell Darryl that he would have to be home around six. His on-line therapy session was starting then, and he wanted to be back in time for it.

The initial session had been helpful in a way that his previous therapist had not been. It was only an introductory session and Paul answered a few questions and typed a paragraph or two of what was bothering him. It was not much; Paul did not know exactly what was bothering him. It was enough, though. The next session would be another on-line chat with the therapist and Paul was looking forward to it. It was not the form he filled out and submitted that made him feel better, it did not delve too deeply. It was what the therapist typed in response while agreeing to the session this evening. "It sounds like you need a vacation."

It sounds like you need a vacation. None of the mumbo-jumbo therapist-speak about the inner mind and "let's talk about your mother" sort of thing. None of that. Right to the point. It sounds like you need a vacation. You need to get away. You need an escape. Exactly.

He heard his brother's truck pull up and he put on his jacket, locked the front door of his house, and climbed into the passenger seat. "Hey, Darryl."

"Pollywog!" Darryl said. Paul did not mind the use of his childhood nickname today. He felt gratitude. "How are you feeling today?"

"Better," Paul said.

"Good to hear, bro." Darryl backed out of the driveway and eased down the street, picking up speed as they left the residential area. "Thanks for helping me out. This won't take much time. I just couldn't spare any guys today. Busy, busy!"

"So, what exactly am I doing?"

"You know the Paradise Manor?" Darryl pulled onto the four-lane heading to the city.

"In Blackburn?"

"No, the complex closer to downtown. The one I bought last year. I bought it and all its tenants?"

"Sure."

"Well, one of the tenants passed away. No next of kin that we can find, there was no emergency contact listed, either. We have to do a bit of moving and cleaning today. You ok with that?"

"No big deal," Paul said. "I have something at six tonight, though, don't forget."

"Yup! We'll be out of there long before then, I just have to get some of the big stuff into the van. Some of my men will be freed up tomorrow. I just need to get the stuff out so the cleaners can come. It's not that much, really. I appreciate it."

"No problem. It's the least I can do," Paul said and Darryl nodded. They rode in silence for a while. "So, who died?" Paul asked.

"What?"

"Which tenant died? Nobody to notify to pick up his stuff? That's shitty."

"No shit, eh?" Darryl said. "An old guy named Gordon Zanders. He lived there a long time."

"Gordon Zanders?" Paul's eyes widened. He recognized a name he had not heard or thought of in maybe twenty years.

"What?" Darryl looked over. "You know him?"

"Well, no," Paul said, "I mean, yes. No, I don't. Not really. Not at all really. You don't remember him?"

Darryl shook his head. "Nope. Should I?"

"Maybe not. You would have been too young, I guess. Dad bought a car from him when I was six. He was a used car salesman and dad bought the car from him on an old lot at the edge of the city, there. I don't even know if it's there anymore."

"No shit." Darryl laughed. "And you remember this?"

Paul remembered when he was young his parents took him to the used car lot at the edge of town when the city was a lot smaller. The car lot, if it still existed, was probably not at the edges anymore, but swallowed up. He did not remember what they were driving when they went in, but he remembered vividly what they drove when they left; a large boat of a car that floated along the potholes and left waves of dust in its wake. It was brown and Paul's family dubbed it The Brown Bug. Paul thought he could remember how to get to the car lot to this very day. He also remembered the red and white triangle flags and their panicked fluttering along the chain link fence that surrounded the lot. There were a lot of cars as well, but he cannot remember individual cars, he can only recall the gleam of them, the sparkle against a blue sky. The parking lot was unpaved and there was a lot of dust. The few cars that drove around the yard made the dust fly, giving the impression that more activity was on than actually was, the illusion that the used car lot was the busiest place in town. Boys from the middle school worked on the weekends to keep the sparkle on the cars. During the week, the customers and salesmen ensured the dust settled again.

More than this, Paul remembered the salesman that helped his father with the decision to purchase the "Brown Bug." Gordon Zanders was one of the few adults that ever spoke to young Paul. It was the first instance Paul recalled where he went from being a non-entity, peeking from under the legs of his father, to a real person with valid thoughts and opinions. Perhaps a person who had as much power in the decision making as his parents. A person the salesman would also have to win over if he were to be successful.

His smile had descended on Paul as warm as his father's hand. Gleaming. "You look thirsty there, young fella'. You thirsty?" He may have even bent down to Paul's eye level.

"Answer, son," Paul's father said.

Did Paul answer? Did Paul even nod? Gordon Zanders stopped what he was doing and disappeared into his office. He came out again with a warm Western Family cola. He opened it and shook the foam off his hand. Paul held the can the entire time they were there. He was empowered, waiting for a chance to speak, and knowing that he never would. Still, if the chance presented itself...

Later, in the office, Paul tried not to look at the calendar on the wall across from the desk. A girl in a bikini. Papers lifted lazily whenever the oscillating fan spun their way. The windows were open, as well. Paul's can of pop was too warm to drink, but he took small sips now and then to show he was still grateful for his gift. The other salesmen shuffled around with their heads down, but Gordon Zanders looked Paul's family in the eyes, always smiling. His attention to Paul's father for the money stuff, a small wink to his mother for the joke stuff, and a smile to Paul for anything left over. When they left, he waved to all three of them; Darryl sat oblivious in his car seat. Paul watched him out the back window of the "Brown Bug." The windows had black wires running through it, which Paul believed was for the radio, he did not know why.

Darryl pulled the truck off the street and into a small parking lot, barely filled with worn out cars. The pavement was cracked and weather-beaten. "This is it?" Paul asked. Paradise Manor consisted of a row of flat-roofed apartments in an L shape around the lot. In fact, seeing it, Paul did not consider them apartments, the place looked like an ancient motel that no one had rented a room in for many years. There were blankets and Canadian flags hanging in the windows in the place of curtains. Old lawn chairs and tired barbecues lined the steps in front of resident's doors. The doors themselves may have been painted at one time but were now sun-scorched and peeling into an unrecognizable array of colour. "My brother is a slum lord," Paul said as he got out of the truck.

"Piss off, man. I don't make a lot of money off this shit hole," Darryl said. "Besides, if it wasn't here, where would these people live? The rent is dirt cheap."

"Oh, you're a philanthropist, all right."

"Dude, fuck off. I'm helping an old dead guy out. No family. I could just take his stuff to the landfill. It's going into storage until I can track someone down that knows him."

"And then?"

Darryl shrugged. "In three months, I'll have an auction."

"Heart of frigging gold, Darryl."

"Cut it out, this is an investment. I have a business to run," Darryl said and opened the door to unit 36. "And let me do the bathroom. I don't want you crawling in the tub and refusing to get out."

"You're a dick," Paul said and entered the dark apartment.

"Gordon Zanders sold my dad a car," Darryl laughed. "Walt Disney was right. It's a small world."

The car lot was not the last place Paul would see Gordon Zanders, though. The city was not so big that it was impossible to see someone occasionally over the course of a few months. Paul would see him when they were out shopping. Paul would walk beside his mother's shopping cart, too old to ride in it, young enough to wish he could, Darryl too small to walk by himself. The shining checkered store tiles were so polished Paul could see the reflection of the light fixtures. Step on only the black tiles for good luck. When they passed Gordon Zanders, Paul would offer an adult hello and the man would nod back. Sometimes smiling, sometimes not if he seemed preoccupied. Those times when Gordon Zanders did not even look at Paul, it would hurt Paul's feelings; he wanted to be remembered. He wanted it known that he was an actual person that had, at one time, occupied a part of Gordon Zanders' daily thoughts. From the car lot, that's right. And how are you today? Fine, Paul might have answered if asked. He would fill the space with stock comments about the weather, maybe. He would try to appear more mature than his years let on.

Gordon Zanders had short stubby fingers with black, wiry hair on the knuckles. He was as wide as he was tall. Perpetually bald and a unibrow. A face that must have been impossible to shave. As Paul grew older and the memory of why he knew this man faded, Paul still said hello to him when they met. Paul would look down on him and the old man would smile even if he did not remember Paul. The greetings were not often. The car lot closed years ago. Gordon Zanders drove the same old car for decades and Paul had no idea what he did for a living or how he got his money. The man had never married. He still stood out for Paul, though. A familiar face. Warmth. He was the first grownup to ever speak to Paul when he was a kid. Eventually Paul forgot the man and his name altogether.

Until today, that is. Until he found out that Gordon Zanders was a tenant in his brother's slum Paradise Manor, the complex with a view that looked out over the roof of Quick Cash Bottle Depot. And that Gordon Zanders had died.

Paul and Darryl cleared out the furniture and television and stacked them in the van parked just outside. The dishes and the single pot were so cracked and worn, they would go in the trash. Darryl left most everything in the bathroom. There was grime on the bathroom mirror and windows and Paul was glad they were not scrubbing those clean. There was a lot of garbage. They stacked the bags in the corner of the now empty living room. Paul was cleaning the utility closet when he found the photograph.

Later, Paul realized he was glad to be the one to find it. That way no one else would ever know. He did not tell Darryl about it; he did not want Gordon Zanders to be mocked posthumously. But he did not throw it away and he did not know why. The photo was from an old instant exposure camera that Paul was sure had no timer, so someone else must have taken the picture for him. Who would take the picture for Gordon Zanders? The man's long fleshy earlobes were adorned with costume jewelry. Makeup. Black hair where a cleavage should have been. Terrible looking hoofs in red high-heeled shoes. Arms at his side, pearl bracelets dangling impotently. Half his smile obscured in a blur of dried mud across the photo.

Paul was not horrified looking at the picture. If anything, he was a little sad. It was a well-kept secret; Paul was sure of that much. Again, at that moment, Gordon Zanders lost his name and became the guy that sold Paul's father a car. He gave Paul a Western Family pop. He spoke to Paul. Now, Paul was the only one to look after this possession. The only one to know his secret. This last possession would not go to the garbage. Darryl needed the apartment cleaned to rent out again because there was always a waiting list for these low-rent rooms. But Paul was keeping this memento for a bit.

"Ok," Darryl said as they climbed into his truck. "Thanks for your help, bro." He held out a hundred-dollar bill to Paul. Paul barked a laugh and shook his head. "No, seriously, Paul, take it. I appreciate the help."

"Darryl, like I said, it's the least I could do. I know I'm a pain in the ass. I don't know what's wrong with me."

"Dude." Darryl's sigh was long and drawn out. "You've always been a little flaky. Ever since we were kids."

"Thanks."

"No insult intended," Darryl said. "Are you taking your pills?" Paul nodded. "Good. See? Today you're ok, right? Are you talking to the doctor?"

"I got referred to an on-line counselling session. That's what I'm doing tonight."

"Like Skype?"

"No, but a closed chat session sort of thing. I don't actually see who I'm talking to. I'm going to give it a go."

"Good, I hope you do," Darryl said, and turned his head away. Paul saw his brother's jaw moving around as if he were chewing. "Because ... well, because..."

"Darryl? Holy shit, man, don't." Was his brother crying?

"I just love you, Pollywog and I am sick of seeing you hurting all the time." Darryl leaned over and wrapped his arms around a surprised Paul. Is this Darryl? Darryl who called everyone bro, male or female. Darryl who watched sports and was known on occasion to smash and throw things if his favourite team did not win? Darryl, who repeatedly told Paul of his and his wife's sex life and inquired about Paul's? Darryl, who, after he let go of his embrace and wiped his eyes and nose with his sleeve, emitted a huge fart and then locked the windows out so Paul could not roll them down.

When Paul logged in to the therapy session later that night, he fully expected to talk about the unexpected brotherly embrace. Or his family. Or any number of things. But it was the photo of Gordon Zanders he wanted to speak about.

: I understand from what you're saying that this had a big impact on you.

: It did. Huge. I have been thinking about it all day.

: Why do you think that is?

: I know why.

: All right. So where is the photo now?

: I kept it. Later I drove down to where the car lot used to be.

The old lot was a compound yard now. There were vehicles there that looked as though they were part of the dirt itself. Weeds appeared magically inside the windshields and through the seats as if they were the souls of the rusty springs. The red and white flags that used to adorn the chain-link fence had made good their escape. The chain-link fence kept nothing of value in and kept no one out. The building looked old and small, each pane of the window where Gordon Zanders office would have been was smashed. Paul wondered if the fan was still inside, shaking its head slowly in disbelief. He rolled up the photo of Gordon Zanders and tucked it through the fence and left without seeing if it had landed face down or face up.

: Something is really bothering you about this photo. Is it the loss of innocence you felt when you saw it? This was someone you always remembered and now you feel as though you remembered him wrong?

: No, nothing like that. It did make me sad for the old man. Carrying that secret.

: But that is not what's really bothering you?

: No.

: Talk it out, Paul, this is what this is all about. What was it?

There was a three-minute pause.

: Paul? Are you there?

: Yes.

: Tell me, Paul. There is no judgement here. It's my job to sort things out with you.

: It's just strange that, of all people, I remembered him so vividly. And then to see that photo. It was like some sort of sign.

: What sort of sign? What do you mean?

: A sign for me that I don't want to have to carry a secret like that forever.

: I see.

: It's like something let loose inside me. And then, l thought, that must be the reason I remembered him so well after all these years.

: And that reason would be?

: I'm afraid of the reason.

: No, you're really not. You have come this far. You are very brave and strong. Tell me.

: It's me. I am like him.

: In what way are you like him, Paul?

: I dress like that, too. In secret. I feel so ashamed and perverted.

: It's not perverted, Paul. And you have nothing to be ashamed of.

: But it's more than just wearing my wife's underwear. I wear her dresses and shoes.

: How often? Never mind, it doesn't matter how often. How does it make you feel?

: At the time? So free.

: Liberated.

:Yes! That's the word! The thing is, that's how I want to dress. Even in public if I could.

: And why shouldn't you? Why couldn't you?

: At work??

: Why not?

: You're kidding.

: I am not making light of this. I understand. It would clear up a lot of trouble for you.

: And cause a lot! I don't want my wife to know. Or my daughter.

: That would be the end of the world?

: I know what you are trying to do, but yes, that would be the end of the world in some sense. The end of our world. And how would I tell my brother?

: If they love you, and I get a sense they do, it will take time but eventually there would be acceptance and then total freedom for you. How would you feel to finally be who you are? To not keep who you are a secret, like Mr. Ganders.

: Zanders.

: Yes, pardon me.

: Family is one thing. How would I tell my boss that I dress and feel like a woman?

: A plan can be made to approach that.

: Not a chance! My boss would fire me!

: First of all, Paul, you cannot be fired for sexual orientation or things of that nature. And second, he may not be my favourite person right now, but I think you would be surprised at how understanding and open-minded Bryce can be.

: What did you say?

No response.

: Hello? What did you say? How did you know my boss's name is Bryce?

No Response.

: Hello?

No response. Beside the blinking cursor: User is off-line. Connection failed.

: Hey!

Reconnection failed.

: Who the fuck is this??

Chapter 6: Warren

With his grandmother in the hospital, Warren could now drink openly in private. He did not have to hide from her in the basement or his room and he could walk around the entire house with the curtains closed, drinking all day. Rather, he could hobble around; crutches and a boot for six weeks. This could not be happening. He hobbled to the liquor store an hour ago and hobbled home with three bottles of spiced rum. The lengths one will go to. It was the most difficult thing he ever had to do. He swore when this was all over, he would go to the clubs and dance every night. He would take Salsa lessons. Get back into floor hockey. The things we take for granted, he thought. He promised he would even take work more seriously when he was able to get back.

There were three reasons Warren was going to celebrate and drink to oblivion tonight, as if he ever needed a reason. One reason was good, one reason was bad, and one reason was very ugly. The ugly reason was the recent and not so quiet meeting with the people he owed a few thousand dollars to which took place earlier. The bad reason was the inevitable conversation with his father, which presented a whole new set of problems. And the good reason was a possible way out of all of it. There was a lot of bullshit that went with it, but if he was smart, he could pull it off. He had to stay sober for a while to keep his head on, but he knew it would work. Could he stay sober? Of course he could. But not tonight. Tonight was for washing all the proverbial dirt away.

The phone call with his father took place earlier, before he was released from Emergency. It went exactly the way he thought it would. Warren called from the hospital and Annette answered. Warren could never call her mom. Or even stepmom, for that matter. "Parker residence, this is Annette Parker." Her voice was still so grating to him even after years.

"I'd like to speak with Jeremy, please," Warren said, looking up into the doctor's smiling face. What was he smiling about? Even the nurses around their station were smiling, leaning away from him, but still refusing to completely give up their post so he could have privacy on the phone.

"I believe Mr. Parker is indisposed at the moment," Annette said, sounding to Warren like an elementary school teacher. "I will take your name and number and make sure he gets it."

"It's Warren, Annette," he said.

"Oh!" Warbly!" Sickly sweet. "I'll get him right now, honey."

Warren covered the receiver and whispered to the nurses and the doctor, "She's getting him right now." More smiling nods. Everyone was head over heels about this phone call, apparently. He could have asked one of the paramedics to go in the house and get his phone before they took him to the hospital, he supposed. Maybe he would have thought that through if it wasn't for the busted leg and intoxication. Still, those pills they gave him were starting to work nicely.

"This is Jeremy Parker," his father said, his voice loud and echoing. Warren knew his father was lounging at home, but he could only ever picture him in his office, suit and tie bulging to bust, cigarette smoldering in an ashtray with a no-smoking symbol painted on the bottom. Curtains drawn against the light as if he was some corporate vampire that only came out at night for meetings.

"Hey," Warren said flatly.

"Yes? Who is speaking, please?" his father said. Warren knew full well Annette would have told him who was calling. Always a power game with this guy, Warren thought.

"It's Warren, dad." He rolled his eyes.

"Well, son." A great exhale of breath. He is just as nervous about this call as I am, the thought flashed through Warren's mind. "What can I do for you, Warren?" His father was speaking again in the harsh tones he had cultivated over the years. Warren's earliest memory was watching father looking at his own reflection in the bathroom mirror, practicing that voice, as if trying to intimidate himself. It had worked on his son if that was any consolation.

"I'm in the hospital, dad."

"What? Are you alright?" Warren could picture the man sitting forward now, veins bulging in his forehead. His face would be red. He would be reaching and fumbling for the solace of a cigarette.

"Nothing. It's nothing. I broke my leg." There were more smiles and nods from the hospital staff. Now I am speaking their language, Warren thought. This is something they understand, pain and fractures and discomfort.

"What happened?" his father asked.

"I fell out of a tree."

"And why were you in a tree?" It was never a genuine question. Always a set up to correct or humiliate.

"Grandma's cat was in it."

"Sugar?"

"Yeah," Warren said. "Grandma was pretty freaked out. She's dead."

"She's what? She's dead? What do you mean? What happened?"

"She was in a tree and..."

"You arsehole," his father interrupted, "I thought you meant my mother was dead."

"Oh, sorry, dad. No. The cat is dead. Sugar," Warren said.

"Well, that is good news." Another sigh. He would be leaning back in his chair now. Warren could picture it all. There would be smoke curling thoughtfully around is head. There would be more grey in his hair, the barber brings out more every time, his father would joke. Or would his hair be thinner? Whatever. Besides, Warren had only been away a year. Not too long in some people's minds. Not long enough in others. Not long enough for his father to change drastically in appearance. Or attitude.

"But that's not why I'm calling," Warren continued.

There was a pause. Warren knew his father was calculating like a chess player trying to anticipate his opponent's move before letting go of his own chess piece he has placed. "You need more money?" His father was tentative.

"You wish," Warren said.

"Why don't you just ask, son..."

"I don't need money," Warren lied. "It's about grandma."

"She needs money?"

"No, she doesn't need money," Warren said. "She's not doing too well. The doctor said..."

"What do you mean, not doing too well? There was a creak of leather and a different tone in his voice. Now Warren knew his father would be leaning forward. Interested now. It was his own mother. Warren thought, maybe his father did care about things other than his career. More than Warren gave the man credit for. Or perhaps the pills were working and making Warren more sympathetic.

"She's... I don't know... she's been acting funny for the last little while."

"We are talking about your grandmother, here." His father emitted an uncharacteristic chuckle.

"More than that, dad," Warren said. "The doctor here is checking her out and he figures she can't be left alone in the house right now."

"But you're there, Warren."

"Well, with my leg, I can't..." Pause. " ...and ..."

"And what?"

"Well, the semester is out soon," Warren said. No response. Warren knew his father could take the bait if he wanted to. The man knew what Warren was getting at. "If I'm laid out with my left, I was thinking about, maybe... you know..."

"I know what?"

"You know, dad," Warren said. "Maybe I could come home for a month or two until..."

"And what about school?" Warren could hear his father breathing through his nose now. The man was disgusted. If only the bastard knew Warren had not been to school in a year. That he was working for minimum wage and not even paying his grandmother rent. If his grandmother was in a home, what the hell would Warren do? His father would sell the house and Warren would need a place to live. If he stayed with his father, the people he owed money to would not bother him there. They were not high-level criminals by any means.

"Just one semester. It's going to be hard with this leg and everything." Warren knew there was more he should say, but the old instinct kicked in. The first one to speak loses, his father had taught him.

Apparently, his father had forgotten his own negotiating rule. "I don't know, Warren," He said. "One semester turns into two. And then you never go back."

"But I will, dad." Warren hated the pleading tone in his own voice. "I'm not going to screw this one up. Ok?"

"And what about grandma?"

"They were talking about a home. They called it the Happy Home of Sunshine. No, the Sunshine Happy... I don't know, something stupid like that. The Sunny Happy..."

"I know the place," his father said. "We took her there once."

"You did? When?"

"Right before you went to school. We took her there just to see. I guess I knew this was coming. I thought it was a better idea for you to stay with her. But now..." Was his father being tender? There was a long pause.

Warren could hear a humming over the miles between them getting louder and louder through the phone. Or was it those painkillers? His father broke the hum, "Do you have to stay there?"

"Where?" Warren said. "At grandma's?"

"No, the hospital. Do you have to stay there?"

"I don't think so? I can ask."

"Don't bother, you probably don't have to stay there. I will put a call in to the nurse's station. I will get you a cab and grandma can stay there for a day or two until I can get things sorted out."

"A cab." Warren's tongue felt thick in his mouth. Already his words were slurring.

"I'll drive down this coming weekend. I'll be there in three or four days." His father's voice was sounding further and further away. "I'll take care of everything."

" ... "

"Warren?"

" ... "

"Warren?" A shout.

"Hey! What?" Warren had only closed his eyes for a second. In that second, he was already home with his dad, He was already in his old bed.

"Just one semester, you got it?" his father said. "What do you plan to do? Are you going to get a job?"

"A job. Yeah."

"I'll pull some strings for you, get the word out."

"Oh, dad, you don't have to do all that..."

"I'll see you in a few days."

Warren did not know whether his father hung up or not. He lay his head on the cool counter of the nurse's station and then found himself being gently lowered into a wheelchair. The vinyl was the most comfortable thing he ever felt. He closed his eyes against the fluorescent light. He began having one of those dreams where he was falling, and he remained just lucid enough to wonder if it was true what they said about hitting the ground before you wake up.

He woke a few hours later and a cab took him home. It turned out he did not have a broken leg. They had mixed up his chart with another young man his age that had been admitted at the same time. He imagined this other poor fellow begging the doctor to take another look; his leg seemed to be broken in two or more places and not merely sprained. Warren was the one with the bad sprain. Still, they fitted him with a different boot and gave him three days of painkillers and, after assuring him his grandmother would be fine, wished him well. Thank you, too, Warren thought as he left.

When the cab dropped him off, the gleam of medication was fading. It was replaced with an ugliness when he saw the front door to his grandmother's house was wide open and all the lights were on in the living room. Through the window he could see three familiar shapes sitting on the couch and the chaise-lounge. Behind him, his only means of escape pulled into the street and was gone in search of another fare.

"What are you doing in my house?" Warren limped in the front door and shouted down the hall.

"Your grandmother's house," came the shouted reply.

Warren hobbled around the corner to the living room. "Ok. What are you doing in my grandmother's house?"

Lance was sitting on the couch, hair slicked back in a baker's net. His plaid shirt was buttoned only at the top and he wore a stained white t-shirt underneath. His dark jeans were too big for him and rode low on his hips. A pair of too white sneakers pointed east and west. Ron was seated next to him, crouched forward, looking at Warren over his glasses. He was fumbling with a crocheted coaster. Jim took up the whole chaise-lounge. He was holding a baseball bat. Shit.

"Ron has been waiting for a call, ese," Lance said.

"I was in the hospital," Warren said. "I fell out of a fucking tree trying to get my grandmother's cat."

"We don't give a shit about nobody's pussy, Holmes. Where the money at?"

"For fuck sakes, Lance," Warren said, still standing. Waiting. "Why are you talking like that these days? You're not even Latino. You're from fucking Saskatchewan."

"You got a problem with Tisdale, Saskatchewan all of the sudden, puta?" Lance stood and stretched his neck to the ceiling, looking down at Warren. To Warren he did not look that menacing. He looked like Lance in a hair net.

"Sit down, Lance," Ron said, tossing the coaster on the coffee table.

"But this pendejo..."

"Sit down!" Ron raised his voice. "He's right, you have been talking in that weird accent a lot these days and it's kind of pissing everyone off. It sounds stupid." To Warren, Ron gestured to his grandmother's rocking chair. Warren shuffled over and sat. He rocked a bit out of habit.

"I can explain," Warren started.

"You better." Ron looked straight at Warren. Of the three men sitting in his grandmother's house, Warren was the most afraid of Ron. His quiet confidence and usual silence were unnerving. Warren had seen Ron beat people without a change of expression. He was glad they were friends, but he knew that could only get him so far. "You owe me $2500," Ron continued in the same, steady tone. "And you haven't been around or returned my calls."

"I know and I'm sorry," Warren said. "It's been crazy with all this stuff with my grandmother lately, we have to put her in a home." No reaction. Damn. They knew his grandmother, too. Ron must be really pissed. "And to be honest, it's $2000. I don't know where this $2500 is coming from. Not that it makes a difference, I know, but that's an extra $500."

"It's $2500, Warren," Ron said.

"No, man, really. Two grand."

Jim spoke up from the chaise-lounge. "We fronted you a thousand bucks worth of product two months ago."

"That's right," Warren said. "And another five hundred in product a few days after that, I'm not saying..."

"And another in $500 cash so you could set up and sell in Edmonton for a week. Did you do that?" Jim placed the baseball bat across his knees.

"No, I didn't go."

"And why not, Warren?" Ron spoke softly.

"But see?" Warren said, holding out his hands. "That's only $2000." He was met with blank stares. "$2000. Don't you keep records of this sort of thing?"

"The wife does," Ron said.

"Well, call Stacy right now," Warren implored. "I swear Ron. Two grand."

"Stacy likes you, Warren," Ron said. "I don't want her to know what we are doing here with you."

Oh, shit.

"We will get to the bottom of this," Ron said. "You still owe the money, and you didn't go north like we told you to."

"I couldn't. I didn't have the product or the cash." He could not tell Ron that he sold the product to pay off some tabs at local bars, paid off Bryce the Boss for a six-month-old loan, went on a weeklong bender and, suddenly, before he knew it, the money was gone. He had seven hundred dollars left. "I can give you $500 right now. I will have to get the other $1500 from somewhere."

"You mean the other $2000 puta," Lance sneered.

"We'll check with Stacy on that," Ron said. "And why didn't you have the product or the cash? Did you spend it? Lose it? Did someone steal it?"

Sunlight poked its way past a cloud in the sky and through a crack in the curtains and lit up the wall across from Warren. Like a sign from God. "That's right." Warren swallowed. "Someone stole it."

Jim stood suddenly from the chaise-lounge and stood over Warren. "I am going to bust up your other leg," he shouted, holding the bat up near the ceiling. Warren rocked in his chair, his scrotum tightening uncomfortably.

"Jim, wait!" Warren shouted. "Ron, tell him. I will get you the money. It was stolen!"

"Tell us one more lie, fuckface!" Jim swung the bat full force into a ceramic lamp on the end table near Warren's head. It smashed against the wall into pieces and Warren covered his eyes.

"Jim! Hey!" Warren said. Oh shit, oh shit, oh shit.

"Hey!" Ron barked. "Sit down Jim. Not cool! That's not his shit, that's his grandma's shit you're fucking up."

"Yeah, Jim, come on," Lance said. "She's a nice old lady. She made us cookies that time, remember?"

Jim stood still and lowered the bat to his side. His face was flushed. He stepped forward and punched Warren in the forehead between the eyes. Warren rocked back, nearly falling over. Jim grabbed the rocking chair and steadied it before sitting back down on the chaise-lounge. Warren had blacked out for a second and held his face. "Ouch, Jim," he said.

"Jimmy wanted to do much worse, Warren," Ron said. "He's not fond of you. He hasn't known you as long as I have. I know you wouldn't purposely screw me over, would you?" Warren shook his head, still holding his face. "Lance had the same idea. But me? I don't know. I trust you. My wife likes you. My kids think you're funny. It would be hard to just..." Ron dropped his head and stared down at the coffee table.

"It wouldn't be hard for me," Jim said.

"Are you being straight up Warren? Did someone steal from us?" Ron asked.

"Yes!" Warren moaned through his fingers. His head was throbbing.

"Who would steal from us, Warren? A stranger? How? No, it must have been someone you knew, right?"

Warren nodded. Oh shit, oh shit.

"Someone you knew, then." Ron nodded slowly, as if commiserating a great tragedy. "What is this person's name? Where is this person right now?"

"That's the thing, Ron. I don't know," Warren said.

"You don't know this person's name?"

"I do know his name. I just don't know where he is." Oh shit. "He hasn't been to work in two weeks." Why was this shit coming out of his mouth? He did not want to be hit again, or worse. Jim looked like he was ready to put him back in the hospital. He needed them to leave so he could buy some time and make a plan. There was always an escape. There was always a way out of any situation you did not want to be in.

"He disappeared?" Jim sneered. "He stole a lousy $2500 and then disappeared? Who does that?"

"Two thousand." Warren said.

"We will check with Stacy on that," Ron countered. "Who was it, Warren. I am done laying around."

"Larry Hansen." Oh shit, for real. "I work with him. I was going to get him to help me unload some of the product and he ripped me off. I wasn't going to tell you because I thought I could take care of it myself. But then he just ghosted me. Then I knew he screwed me over."

Ron ran his fingers through his hair and let out an exasperated sigh. "It's hard to believe, Warren."

"Ya, Warren," Lance said. "It's not like we're the Mexican cartel, here, ese. No one disappears over $2500."

"It's two grand."

"Whatever," Ron said and drummed his fingers on the coffee table, his eyes boring a hole in Warren's head. Warren tried his best to return the stare. He cannot know I'm lying, he thought. Ron squinted. "I am not just writing this off. Warren."

"Of course."

"He hasn't been to work in two weeks? You don't know where he is?"

"No."

"I want my money, Warren."

"I know, man. I'm as pissed off as you are. I got ripped off, man. Now I'm in trouble because of this dickhead? Give me some time to find him and I will get your money back." Even to Warren's ears this sounded convincing.

"You look for him," Ron said and, as if he had given some silent cue, all three men stood. "And we are going to look for him, too."

Good luck with that, Warren thought. Not even his wife knows where he went. She has been to the office three times already talking to Bryce the Boss. Warren had even seen Larry Hansen's wife with Bryce in his car in the parking lot at work. She has probably been to the police twice that many times. Where could he have gone?

"And answer your phone when I call." Ron said as they were leaving. "Do not keep me guessing."

"I won't Ron, I promise."

Wait. Larry Hansen's wife sitting in Bryce's car? Her coming to see Bryce? Did they know each other that well? Hold on a second. Before the revelation could fully take form in Warren's mind, Lance punched him in the side of the head. Then they left.

Warren needed a drink. Lance's punch was nowhere near as hard as Jim's. But still.

Chapter 7: Bryce Springsteen

I did not want to blindside the group with an unexpected police visit, so I arranged for the whole office to gather in the boardroom for a quick meeting. We had never been in the boardroom all at once; usually it was a meeting for sales, a separate meeting for accounting, or another for administration. I needed to address everyone. I had extra chairs brought in, but some still had to stand against the wall. I was going to explain carefully what was happening. I anticipated this would be stressful for some people, and I needed everyone happy, comfortable, and relaxed. I promised to make it quick.

"Thank you for coming," I said to the group once they were settled, and the murmur of conversation died down. It was not as if they had an option for coming in, but I wanted them to think they were doing me a favour. As Bryce and not The Boss. "I wanted to let you all know that starting today and over the next few days, and I'm not sure exactly when, but the RCMP will be in and have requested to speak with us all individually."

"What happened? Are we in trouble?" one of the sales reps at the back of the room asked. I can never remember the sales reps names. "Is someone stealing?"

"Well, no," I said. "Why would you ask that?" Why would he jump right to that conclusion? I would have to talk with him later.

"Just wondering," He said and sank in his seat out of sight.

"No, this is regarding Larry." Silent stares from the room. "Larry Hansen in administration?" This was met with collective recognition and nods.

Just then, the door to the boardroom opened and Warren stood in the frame. He had two black eyes and a nasty bruise on the side of his head and crutches under his arms. "Sorry I'm late," he said, and limped in, knocking into chairs and saying excuse me, excuse me. One of his crutches crunched Jenny's toes and Jeff (her cousin? Her boyfriend?) said, "Watch it, Warren!"

"Ya, I'm kind of on crutches here, Jeff?" Warren said. Paul was kind enough to give up his seat and Warren slumped into it, relieved. He was sweating hard.

"Rough weekend, Warren?" someone asked and the room tittered. How many times had I asked Warren the same question?

"You could say that," he said.

"As I was saying…" I had to start again, "the police will be requesting to interview everyone today and for the next few days, however long it takes. Some of you did not even know Larry, so the interviews should be quick."

"What do they want to talk to us about?" This came from Lisa, looking bored and distant as usual.

"He has been gone a while and no one knows where he is." I had to be firm and direct with Lisa, and never show weakness. She was the mayor's wife and did not need this job. There was no reason for her to have the attitude she did, but I vowed to myself to treat her as I did anyone else. She would not bully me as she did the others.

"Not even his wife?" Warren asked, tilting his head and staring straight at me. Warren tended to avoid all eye contact when he was hung over and I did not like the way he was looking at me now.

"If Marie knew, Larry would not be missing, now, would he? And the police would not be looking for him, would they, Warren?" Damn. Did I just use Marie's name? That's not so unusual, is it? Should I have just said Larry's wife? Or Mrs. Hansen? Using her name made it sound as though we knew each other. We did know each other, but these people did not need to know that. They should not know that. They better not know. How could they know?

"It is weird," Paul said from the corner. "Two weeks now. Longer?"

"Yes, more than two weeks now," I said softly. I treated Paul in the direct inverse of how I treated Lisa. Paul was sensitive and I always felt I had to be gentle. Still, I was grateful he came in for this meeting. He had booked time off for personal reasons, but I knew what that meant. Another meltdown. He was such a likeable guy, but so high maintenance. And today, was he wearing lipstick? It looked like he was wearing lipstick. Chapstick, maybe. "As I said," I continued, "the interviews will start today with the people that worked with him on a day-to-day basis. That would be myself, Jeffrey, Jenny, Marcus, Paul, Lisa, Derrick, and Warren."

"Today?" Warren said. "This is garbage."

"It's not up to me and it can't be helped." The little shit was always complaining. "If anyone feels more comfortable, they have agreed to allow me to sit in on any or all of these interviews. This is not a big deal, guys. He is missing and they just want him found. We all do. None of us had anything to do with his disappearance."

"What reason would any of us have anything to do with his disappearance, Bryce?" Warren asked. All eyes in the room went to him for his question, and then back to me for the answer.

"Well, obviously no reason, Warren," I said.

"Can you sit in with my interview, Bryce?" Paul spoke up.

"Of course, Paul. And like I said, if anyone else wants me to sit in with them, I would be fine doing so. This is just procedure, and they just want to know who Larry was. I mean who he is, his habits, his friends and co-workers. Nothing to be alarmed or nervous about." Some of them did look nervous, though. I was a bit nervous myself. "Now, let's get back to work. I will call on you when you're needed, and I will try to give you a fifteen-minute heads up. Like I say, this is not a big deal, I just want to find out what happened to Larry and if he is ok. Anything we can do to help will be greatly appreciated. And Marie will be happy that we assisted." For crying out loud, I used her name again.

They filed out of the boardroom, gossiping, and laughing and bumping into each other to get through the doorway first. Warren, because of his crutches, was last. "Can I see you in my office?" I said to him as he hobbled past.

"Sure."

I followed him down the hall to my office. It was very slow, and I shuffled behind him. I felt like an idiot. I should have walked in front. Was he being deliberately slow? It was hard to tell, he did have that boot on. I helped him get settled in a chair and then I walked around to sit at my desk opposite him. "What the hell, Warren?" I said.

"What?"

"What, what?" Unbelievable. "What do you mean, what? You look like you got hit by a bus. What happened?"

"I had some trouble with my grandmother's cat," he said.

I held up my hands asking him to expand on that. He just stared at me. "And?"

"And that's it."

"Your grandmother's cat beat the crap out of you?" I said. "I can't afford any more time off from you, Warren. And now Paul is off for a week. And Larry..."

"Yes, Larry. Very strange, isn't it?" He was smiling at me. Why would he be smiling about a missing person?

"Something amusing you?" I asked. I could feel the blood rushing to my face. I did not like speaking with Warren in private. He was the type of employee that made you feel that punching someone in the face and being sued was not a bad option.

"I need some money, Bryce," he said, flatly.

"All right," I said. He had never been so direct before. I had loaned him twenty dollars before. Once three hundred, which he was slow to repay, but he did pay me back. But he had asked in all humility then. Never so brazen. There was something going on. "I can ask accounting to give you an advance."

"No, not an advance. I need it from you." That smile.

"You need a loan?" I asked. "What for? How much? Fifty?"

"$2000," he said. "No, $2500."

My mouth dropped. "Twenty-five hundred dollars? Are you kidding me? I can't lend you twenty-five hundred dollars."

"I didn't say lend." The little shit was still smiling. "I said I need twenty-five hundred bucks from you."

"What the hell are you talking about, Warren? I can't give you twenty-five hundred bucks. Why would I just give you twenty-five hundred bucks?"

He moved his boot a little to the side and seemed to be getting more comfortable. "The police are coming to interview everyone, what? Today?" he said.

"Some today?" I frowned. "Why?"

"Well, they can talk to me if they want, but I don't know anything about anything. I barely know the guy and I have no idea where he is."

"I know that."

"But maybe I can tell them something that can help them out." His smile vanished.

"So... what? You do know something about Larry?" I was confused now.

"I don't know anything about Larry. But I know something about you." He let the silence between us hang. And then, "Are you screwing Larry's wife, Bryce?"

I said, "What?" Smaller and higher pitched than I should have. It was drawn out, like: whaaaaat? "Marie?" Damn. I used her first name again. My cheeks flushed. I am a terrible liar.

"Yes, Marie. You heard me. Are you sleeping with her?"

"I don't know what you're talking about," I said.

"I'm talking about I want twenty-five hundred bucks and I don't say anything to the cops."

"What the hell would you have to say to the cops, Warren?"

"That you were screwing his wife."

"I am not screwing Marie." Could I stop fucking using her first name?

"Listen, Bryce…" Warren struggled to stand and get his crutches under his arms. He looked like a raccoon with those two black eyes. That must have been one hell of a scrap with his grandmother's cat. There must be more to that story. There always is with Warren. And now this. "I'm in a bind and I need that money. You give me the cash and I don't say anything about you and Marie. I quit this stupid job and go live with my dad in Ontario. You don't give me the money and I tell the cops about your affair and shit gets really uncomfortable for you. They will be looking at you real closely and they won't leave you alone. And everyone will know."

"You little shit," I said. He was already more than fired from his stupid job.

"It's not personal, Bryce."

"It sounds pretty damn personal, Warren." It was all I could do to keep from leaping over the desk and beating the shit out of this little, drunken, useless, mouthy…

My intercom buzzed. "Mr. Springsteen?"

I punched the intercom instead of Warren. "Yes, what is it? I'm in a meeting."

"The police are here, and they would like to speak with Paul."

"I will be right out." Then to Warren: "Don't do anything. I had nothing to do with Larry disappearing."

But that felt like a lie. "I was not sleeping with his wife." That was definitely a lie.

"I'll send you a text," Warren said and I followed him out to the foyer. I watched him limp out the office doors to the elevator. He did not even ask or imply that he was taking the day off. That little shit. Sure, he was in a cast or a boot or whatever they call those things. But, the nerve.

There were two men in suits standing at the reception desk. The first was only a few inches taller than I am but seemed to tower over me. His shoes were polished perfectly and his pants ironed. His suit was fresh and the belt and holster holding his gun looked as though they were part of him. His impeccable white shirt stretched over his chest, you could tell the man was fit, and his jacket fit snug around his broad shoulders. His nose was straight, and his symmetrical eyes were an impossible light blue, set off more so by the silver streaks in his hair, which was manicured to a manly perfection. He had just the right amount of stubble on his square, movie star jawline. His partner was shorter, and it looked as though his uniform was a size too big.

The tall, better-looking officer spoke first. "Good afternoon, I'm Detective Coxcomb and this is Detective Thorpe. Thank you for taking the time to meet with us."

I shook both their hands. "Hello. I'm Bryce Springsteen."

"Ha! Really?" The shorter office laughed, and I frowned. "I meant no offence. It's just... Bryce Springsteen? You must have been teased a lot." The good-looking officer gave his partner a look that shut him up and I showed them the way to my office, calling over my shoulder for my receptionist to send Paul in.

"Again, thank you for seeing us," Detective Coxcomb said once we were settled in our chairs. "I know this must be difficult for you and your staff. I just want you to be assured that we are working diligently on this case and I believe we are going to come to a satisfactory conclusion."

"We are praying for a happy ending," I said.

"Hmph!" Thorpe tried to suppress a laugh. "Happy ending," he mumbled. He received another look from Coxcomb. Were they partners or was Coxcomb his superior? The good-looking officer certainly carried himself as if he were in charge. His expression never changed, and I felt like he was scrutinizing my every change of tone and mannerism. His partner had started playing with my Zen garden.

Paul knocked softly on the door and waited even though the timid bugger knew he was expected. I waved him in and he pulled a chair from the corner and sat with his knees together. It really did look like he was wearing lipstick in this light. Not heavy lipstick, but like Marie's lipstick after it had been a bit worn thin after they had... no. No, stop thinking about that.

"Paul, thank you for meeting with us," Coxcomb said. "This is just a formality. We want to talk with people who knew Mr. Hansen and see if we can get a handle on where he may have gone."

"Do you think he's dead?" Paul asked.

"Do you think he's dead?" Thorpe set down the Zen rake and leaned forward, suddenly interested in Paul.

The good-looking officer held both his hands in the air, trying to regain his control. "No, we do not believe Mr. Hansen is deceased." He glared at Thorpe and his partner seemed to shrink back in his chair. "Were you close?" Coxcomb asked Paul.

"No, I wouldn't say that," Paul said. "We worked together. I had been to his house a few times."

"And you knew his wife?"

"No, he didn't know Marie," I stuttered and laughed nervously. "You didn't know Marie, did you, Paul? None of us really know Marie." Both officers were looking at me. Why did I interrupt?

"No, not really," Paul said. "I met her, of course, but I didn't really know her."

"I mean... haha! Only a husband can really know his wife, am I right?" *Shut up, Bryce. What the actual fuck here?*

Thankfully, I was ignored as the good-looking officer leaned forward in his chair and looked into Paul's eyes. "Paul," He said softly, and I could see Paul visibly relax. He did not feel threatened. Until: "I have a reason to believe that you have been in recent contact with Mr. Hansen."

Paul's mouth fell open and I could see in his eyes he was about to have one of his episodes. It happened regularly. A simple scrape on his car would send him panicked into the washroom and I would have to talk him into coming out, while listening to him moan, "Screw my life, screw my life." Good guy. Great employee. But so high maintenance. The look on his face was one I had seen before.

"What? I never... what? I haven't seen Larry..." His lower lipsticked lip began to quiver.

I had to jump in. "No, this isn't possible."

"Why do you say that?" Thorpe shot me a glance. There was no longer any humour in that look.

"If Paul had been in contact with Larry, he would have told us. I mean, we are all concerned. His wife is so worried she can't sleep at night." *Fuck sakes, why don't I just whip out my phone right now and show them all the sexting.*

"Paul," The good-looking officer pulled a business card and a pen from his front pocket. He wrote something on the back of the card and slid it in front of Paul. "Do you recognize this website?"

Paul's face went pale, and his eyes widened as he looked at the business card. I felt a small bit of sweat on my brow. Oh, my God. He knew something. Paul knew something about Larry's disappearance. "Paul?" I ventured.

"I do recognize that, yes," Paul said, very weak and small. Smaller than usual, even.

"And have you had any interaction on this website. Have you communicated with someone on this website?" The good-looking officer asked gently.

"Yes."

"Have you spoken with this person directly? On the phone, perhaps?"

"No."

"On a webcam, maybe? Skype?"

"No."

"So, just a webchat?" The good-looking officer was leaning toward Paul. Not in a menacing way, but in a nurturing way. I thought maybe he would even put a reassuring hand on Paul's knee.

"Yes, just a webchat. Not in person." Paul's voice was shrinking and shrinking.

"How many times, Paul?"

"Twice."

"Three times, perhaps?" Coxcomb asked.

"Yes, ok. Maybe it was three times," Paul said. "I didn't do anything wrong." I could see him folding in on himself and I felt the urge, as I always did with Paul, to either comfort him or shake the shit out of him.

Both detectives leaned back in the chairs at the same time, causing me to relax and lean back as well. I had no idea what I was witnessing, here. "You're not in any trouble," Thorpe said. The kindest he had been since he walked in.

"I'm not?" Paul said. "I don't know anything about Larry. I don't know where he is. I swear."

"It's fine, Paul," Coxcomb said. He reached up and smoothed his already perfect hair. "This website is operated by a Dr. Larry Hansen. He lives here in the city, but his friends and family are all on the coast. They have not heard from him in four weeks. Suddenly, the website becomes active again, but still his family have not heard from him. Strange."

"I don't understand," Paul said. I wasn't following either, but I didn't want to say anything. "What does that mean?"

"We're not sure what it means, to be honest. But we cross-referenced the interactions on the website and your name came up through your URL. And then another Larry Hansen was reported missing two weeks ago, around the same time the website started reporting activity again." Coxcomb paused and put his hand on Paul's shoulder. "Who did you think you were talking to, Paul?"

"A doctor? A therapist?" Paul squeaked.

"I believe you," Coxcomb said.

"Well, sure we believe you," Officer Thorpe spoke up. "But, you know, don't, like, leave town or anything."

The good-looking officer winced. "Yes, of course, we will want to speak with you again, so tell me if you have a trip planned."

"I don't have a trip planned," Paul said.

"Good."

"Wait," I said. I was confused. "So, you're saying there are two Larry Hansen's? And they are both missing? Two?"

Chapter 8: Larry Hansen

Larry Hansen read about his disappearance like everyone else: in the morning paper. The announcement was in the Police Beat section on page three, tucked in between an attempted mugging and a credit card fraud. He read it twice.

He heard his wife roll out of bed and shuffle down the hall. He listened as she used the washroom, her urinating echoing off the tile. He pushed the folded paper to where she would sit. Marie slid to the coffee machine and poured herself a cup. Her housecoat hung on her skeletal shoulders and her hair clung in strands to her face. She hid herself behind her steaming cup in front of the paper.

"Did you see that?" Larry said.

"Mmm-mmmm."

"I'm in the paper." He smiled.

"Sluurp."

"It must be a mistake, or something."

"..."

"It says," he cleared his throat and fell into his reading voice, "Larry Hansen, reported missing Thursday, October 15. Last seen in Buck's Bistro. Wearing black slacks and a blue sweater. Anyone knowing of his whereabouts is asked to contact the local department... detachment of... it goes on like that." He set the paper in front of Marie again, thinking she would pick it up. She did not.

"Hmphh..." she said. "Sluurp."

"What do you think of that?"

"..."

"I know, I know." He shook his head and shrugged.

Larry finished his coffee and folded the paper under his arm. "I'm off." He kissed Marie's cheek on the way out. In the garage he depressed the button on his keypad to open the overhead door. The door was halfway up with the sun peeking through when Larry noticed the flat tire. "Great." He said. He opened the trunk and, after a few minutes of fighting, bounced the spare tire on the garage floor. By the time he finished changing the tire there was grease on his shirt and tie. He was twenty minutes late for work.

Larry found his wife on the phone when he went back into the kitchen. She stared at him with wide eyes and held the phone to him. "It's Bryce," she said.

"Oh?" He took the receiver from her. "Bryce?"

"What? Larry?" Bryce said.

"Hey, Bryce. I know... I know, I'm late. I had a flat. Can you tell Jeff or Jenny I'll be there in about fifteen?"

"No problemo, buddy," Bryce said.

"I have something to show you," Larry said, "in the paper this morning. It says I'm missing."

"In today's paper?"

"Weirdest thing. Did you read it?"

"No," Bryce said, "who reads the paper these days?"

"I'll bring it in," Larry said.

Marie was pasted against the far kitchen wall when he hung up the phone. "Are you feeling Ok?" He asked as he passed her.

"Mm-hmmm," she said.

Larry changed his shirt and tie. He jotted down a reminder to himself to get the flat tire fixed later, preferably that day. He missed the rush hour traffic by half an hour but had to park further from the office than usual.

There was a pile of unfinished paperwork on his desk when he arrived. He began to sift through it when Jeff and Jenny walked by his cubicle, side by side. Larry shouted to catch them. "Sorry I'm late. Flat tire."

"You were late?" Jeff slowed and hung to the edge of the cubicle, half his body looking as though it was still moving away.

"Flat tire," Larry shrugged.

"That's funny, we didn't even notice." Jeff looked at Larry's desk. "I was wondering why all the stuff I was leaving you wasn't coming back through. Anyway, double your pleasure in the workload today. The Boss Bryce Springsteen called in sick. If you can't finish by five..." Jeff waved his arm around the office, "anyone else here can do it."

"That's funny, I just talked to him," Larry said, but Jeff and Jenny were gone.

The paperwork was there and would not go away. Trips to the coffee machine only put it off, it was always waiting for him when he returned. He must put a check mark in three places where the information was correct, where the information was not correct, he must correlate it to another form that would correct the mistake. These corrections must match a duplicate file on a line that corrected the correction. If any of this was not done in the proper order, the coupons would not be validated, costing the company hundreds of dollars.

Jenny returned to his cubicle just before noon. "How's it going, Barry?"

"Larry."

"How's it going, Larry?"

"Fine. I hope I'm done by five."

"Are you ok?" It was as though Jenny had not heard what he said. She was looking at Larry more intently than he ever remembered her doing. "You look like crap."

"I don't feel like crap."

"Your eyes. Holy crap, man, have you been sleeping?"

Larry shrugged, "Fine as far as I know. Maybe a couple late nights. Early mornings. I don't know."

"Are you hot?" Jenny came right into the cubicle. It was something she had never done. Larry was glad he cleaned his workplace.

"I'm fine, really."

"You're sweating."

"I'm fine."

"Listen, you should go home." Jenny said, lifting the remaining pile of coupon validation forms from Larry's desk. "Jeff?" she called over the cubicle wall.

"Yes?" came the muffled reply.

"Shred these." Jenny passed the pile over the cubicle wall to a hairy hand.

"Will do."

"You go home, now." Jenny turned to Larry. "You look like crap. See a doctor."

"Well, there really is a lot of work to do." Larry said. "If I lose a day, I don't know... "

"You're kidding, right?" Jenny smiled. "Listen, Barry, we can handle... "

"Larry."

"Larry," Jenny put her hand on Larry's shoulder, "Go home. Jeff and I will cover for you."

But Larry did not go home. He ate his lunch and read his paper in the lunchroom, waiting for someone to come in. In a few minutes, Paul shuffled in and looked through the fridge, settling on a slice of apple pie. Larry shoved the paper across to him when he sat down.

"What?" Paul asked.

"I'm missing," Larry said, smugly.

"What?"

"Look at page three." Larry smiled.

"Why don't you just read it to me," Paul said.

Larry read the police announcement. "What do you think of that?" he said.

Paul shrugged. "Typo?"

"Yeah, but I mean, it's not everyday you find your name in the paper saying you're missing and everything."

"It's just a typo."

"I could phone the paper, I suppose," Larry said.

"Sure."

"A person should straighten something like this out, eh?"

"I guess," Paul said. "Sure." He scooped up his pie and ducked out of the lunchroom.

Larry used the telephone on his desk back at his cubicle. "Hello, I have a complaint to make about something I read in the Police Beat today. In this morning's paper. Not a complaint, really, but like a retraction. I have to make a retraction. *You* have to make a retraction. On a mistake. Or a misprint. A typo."

"I'm sorry, sir. What do you want?" the receptionist on the line said. "A classified error?"

"Well, no," Larry said. "In the Police Beat this morning it said that I was missing. And I'm not. I mean, you can never be missing from yourself, really, because everywhere you go... poof... there you are." Larry's laugh snorted as it occasionally did. "But here I am at work and I'm not missing. You know... everything's cool."

"Police Beat?"

"You know, on page three."

"I know what it is," the receptionist said. "But we get those from the cops, we don't write those out ourselves."

"Maybe it was a typo then?"

"Hardly."

"Maybe it was a police error?" Larry said.

"Maybe."

"Maybe I should phone them, then?"

"Maybe you should go down there in person," the receptionist said. "Then they'll see you're not missing, because... poof... there you'll be."

Larry agreed and stopped by Jenny's cubicle on the way out. She waved him off without looking up from her desk. Where else could a person have a job with such flexibility, Larry thought as he rode the elevator to the ground floor.

The police station was thirty-eight blocks from work with several detours for construction. Larry gripped the steering wheel, only releasing it to return the middle finger to other angry motorists. Thankfully, the police parking lot was not full.

"My name is Larry Hansen," Larry said to the officer at the front desk.

"What can I do for you?"

"Larry Hansen?" Larry smiled a knowing smile.

"Ok... how can I help you?" A slight frown. "Are you feeling alright?"

"I'm Larry Hansen," he repeated. "This morning in the paper you said I was missing." Larry passed the folded paper across the desk. The announcement in question was highlighted with a yellow marker.

The officer read it over and looked up at Larry. "You're Larry Hansen?"

"Yes." Larry reached into his jacket for his wallet. He flipped it open to expose his driver's license. The officer inspected the picture.

"You had hair, here," he said.

"I shaved it off."

"You shaved it off? Lose a bet?" the officer said. Larry did not smile back. "Why did you shave it off?"

"I don't know. Tired of it."

"Tired of it? Really?" the officer ran his fingers through his own hair.

"Sometimes I couldn't face combing it." Larry frowned. Now he could not remember why he had shaved. "You know, in the morning."

"It looks nice here." The officer compared the license to Larry's face. "A little grey, but... " He cleared his throat and handed Larry his wallet. "Well, you're obviously not missing."

"No."

"Hang on a second." The officer disappeared into a back office. Larry drummed his fingers on the desk. He felt the stubble on his head and scratched at it. Why had he shaved? Some days he forgot and would be surprised by his own reflection in the mirror. The developing double chin, the deep lines under his eyes. Sometimes it was as though he were missing. Where did he go?

On the side wall a bulletin board displayed images of people that were missing for real. Most of the photos were of young people. It was just more proof; men forty years old do not go missing for any reason. It was a misprint.

The officer appeared with a sheet of paper. "Ok, here we go." He placed it on the desk but shielded it when Larry tried to look.

"It was a misprint?"

"No, strangest thing, though," the officer said. "His family reported him missing to his company and his employer contacted us."

"But that's not me, right?"

"No, but it's the same name. Larry Hansen. See?" The officer held his hand over the sheet of paper so Larry could only read the name. "Same name," the officer said, once he was satisfied Larry had seen all he needed to see.

"That's weird," Larry said. "I've lived here for eight years and I've never heard of this guy."

"Well, it's not so strange," The officer said. He reached for a phone directory. There was an old-style red rotary phone with buttons instead of a dial. The officer pushed it to the side and flipped through the pages of the phone book. "There." The officer tapped a smudged white page. Larry slid his hand over the book. His name was printed twice, each with a different address and phone number. Larry did not realize they still printed phone books.

"No way. I never knew. That is bizarre."

"Bizarre that you never knew? I mean, people have the same names all the time."

"You?"

"Well, no, but it happens. I mean, well, I don't know anyone personally, but it must happen all the time. It must not be that uncommon."

"I guess," Larry said. He pulled the phone to him and lifted the receiver. He held it out to the officer for permission and the officer shrugged. Larry dialed the number listed. There was a click after four rings. "An answering machine," he whispered to the officer.

"Well, it would be," the officer said. "He's missing, right?"

"You have reached Dr. Larry Hansen," the recorded voice mumbled to him. "I am unavailable to take your call at the moment, if you would care to leave a message, please do so after the beep." BEEP.

Larry considered leaving a message but changed his mind and placed the receiver back in its cradle. "Have you been over to his place?"

"Probably? At this stage they spoke to his relatives, I'm sure. His employer, as well. So far, nothing. People his age, your age, they go through things sometimes and they take off for a while..."

"Where does he work? Where did he work?"

"He's not dead, you know," the officer laughed. "I don't think."

"I didn't say he was."

"Well, it's just the way you said it, 'where did he work.'" Another laugh. "Some e-business thing. From his home, I believe. An on-line chatty thing. I'm not really sure, I'm not the officer that..."

"Well, thanks," Larry said and took his paper.

"Have a nice day."

The street led Larry toward home, but coming home midafternoon was foreign to him. He was waiting for the sky to get dark. For the streetlights to wake up and shine ineffectively. For the cityscape to dress itself in its evening wear in the distance. But midafternoon traffic was laid back and lazy. The radio was all talk. There were plenty of children out on his block, now coming home from school. He did not realize there were so many children in his neighborhood, he had never seen them before. His boss's car was in his drive when he arrived home.

"Bryce?" Larry whispered as he edged the car in near his boss's vehicle. The tires slipped from the drive into the flowerbed. "What are you doing here?" But he knew. He knew. He had known for a while, maybe. There were no words to put to it; Bryce's car in the drive was all the word-picture he needed. It made sense. He felt more relief at that moment than anger. A thing confirmed always brings relief. Otherwise, the questions and doubt would haunt you. He had known since the Charades party. It was the way she looked at Bryce so intently when he guessed Lisa pretending to be that one-armed drummer.

Larry sat in the car letting the heat from the afternoon build up on him. He waited for the injustice of the situation to take hold. He waited for the righteous anger. But there was nothing. Mostly he felt tired. The day, the paper, the flat tire... it was more in one day than he cared to face. And now this, but it seemed fitting and right. Phase three in Larry's life, in which he no longer exists. Missing, just like the paper said. It had not been a misprint after all. The other Larry Hansen, the actual one that was missing, he knew what it was all about, the futility, the boredom. Or maybe he was dead. Which was more appealing sometimes. To get out while the getting was good.

They were sleeping in his bed when he found them. They looked so happy he did not want to disturb them. There would be a scene if he did. There would be anger, and blame, and yelling, and something would have to be done. He was thirsty. He took a drink from a half empty glass of water on the nightstand. He noticed the alarm clock was set and he tested the time. It was set for four-forty-five, enough time for Bryce to be gone. Marie would have made the bed and supper for Larry when he came home. He conceded this was thoughtful of them. He could leave, he supposed, but where would he go? He did not have the energy for a divorce. He did not have the energy to find another job and new friends. Regardless, he would have to take some personal time away from work now. But what would he do? Maybe he could leave for a little while.

Larry found a small suitcase in the spare room and tiptoed around the sleeping lovers. He picked out socks, underwear, shirts, dress pants, toiletries. He filled a Thermos full of fresh coffee. He tossed the suitcase in his backseat and edged past Bryce's car.

After a short nap in a hotel room, he called his wife. "Where are you?" she said.

"I got off work early." he said.

"..."

"It's ok, you know. I sort of knew."

"Larry, I'm sorry," she said. "We didn't mean to. And it's over."

"I might be gone for a while, but I didn't pack enough stuff. Can I use the credit cards?"

"There's room," she said. "But wait. Please don't hang up. I don't know what to say. I didn't mean for this to happen."

"You don't have to say anything. I'm ok with it, I really am. I'm just going to take a break, and..."

"That's just it," Marie said. "You have been taking a break for the last six months. You don't talk. You stare at the TV..."

"I like a little television when I get home from work."

"That would be fine, but you don't turn it on. You just stare at it. Bryce told me that you have stopped doing anything at work, too."

"What work?" he spat, suddenly angry. "I don't do anything. Anyone else could do that job, Jeff and Jenny said so themselves. No one would even notice when I'm gone."

"Don't say that." She was starting to cry. "You're not going to do anything stupid are you?"

"Like what?"

"You know what."

"Well, no I don't, but..." He closed his eyes. It felt nice and his mind floated for a while with the buzz from the phone so close to his ear.

"Larry?"

"..."

"Larry?" she pleaded. That bothered him. It was like the horn of a boat on this calm water. He let the phone fall from his shoulder. He could still hear the horn, distant now, but still there. He yanked the phone cord hard and then there was nothing.

He woke thinking he could not breathe. It was the hotel's phone book, fat and heavy, lying on his chest. It was open to H. He found the two names, one his own, one belonging to a person he did not know existed before today. Strange. The address was across town, but he had nothing but time, now.

He got lost twice before finding the proper street. The neighborhood was similar to his own; not upscale, but not poor either. The house was smaller than his and the paint was peeling, and the lawn was neglected. Still, it did not look completely abandoned. No one answered the doorbell. He could hear it chiming inside the house. The door was locked, of course.

The day was hot and bright, but the neighborhood seemed deserted as Larry walked around the side of the house into the shade of the trees in the back yard. The grass there was as long as the lawn out front. The wooden steps to the back door were falling apart. There was a note taped to the handle of the door. "I was here" it read, with the letter "F" as a signature. Larry knocked with his fist, rattling the window in the door. Nothing. He knocked again. He waited and then stepped back off the step.

What was he doing here? He should leave and just go home. Go back to work and pretend he did not know anything about his wife and his boss. Or go back to his career at Consumer Life and make believe he believed in it like he did before. Or maybe a quick holiday. Escape somewhere nice.

From the corner of his eye, he noticed that a basement window was open a crack. He managed to slip his fingers through the opening, and to his surprise, it slid open. He pulled his body through the window and balanced his hands on the cool surface of a washing machine, dragging his legs through behind him. The basement was unfinished, and the cement was cracking, there was a faint mildew smell. A string attached to the light bulb in the ceiling proved useless when he pulled it. "Hello?" He walked the perimeter in the half-light, finally finding stairs leading up. With every step up the stairs he called out, "Hello?" Step. "Anyone at home?" Step. "Larry Hansen?" Step. "You're not going to believe this." Step.

The basement door opened to the kitchen on the main floor. It was clean, for the most part. To Larry, it did not look absolutely lived in, but it did not look as though someone was on an extended vacation, either. In the living room the television was on with the sound down. A telephone was on a table beside the couch. Near the phone, an answering machine blinked the number 24 in a small frantic red display. Larry pressed the button marked "PLAY."

A choppy voice told him that there were "twenty-three new messages and one old message." The messages began to play out. The old message was a telephone solicitor offering theatre tickets. The new messages were from family members and a man named Frank, whom Larry assumed was an employer. "You are not answering e-mails." The first few messages sounded relatively light and cheerful, then a little more urgent.

"Call me when you get home, things are starting to back up." "I'm coming over there." Then frightened, "I've called the police. Call me when you can. Please let me know you're alright."

Larry stopped the messages. He crossed the living room and turned the TV off. Outside, the branches of trees in the front yard tapped gently on the window.

The dresser drawers in the bedroom were standing open and empty. The closet, too, had been stripped, leaving only the hangers waiting for anyone's return. On a small desk a large computer let out an authoritative hum. Across the desk were printouts from e-mails with handwritten messages scrawled over them. Larry glanced at one, it read like an advice column; someone was having trouble telling their brother-in-law to move out of their home. Handwritten across the letter was a note to look up a particular bible verse and a note of encouragement. Similar papers filled the desk and made a trail to a small filing cabinet. Larry slid the drawers open. A-F. The next drawer: G-M. An e-business? Is that what the officer had told him? How on earth did that work? Was it...

BING-BONG.

The doorbell broke through the quiet of the room and Larry jumped, then froze. There was a ringing in his ears and the bell sounded again. Guilt goaded him to leave the bedroom and he tiptoed down the hall, his back against the wall. In the living room he stayed close to the floor, peaking through the window. A shadow swayed back and forth there. Larry saw a hand hesitating at the doorbell and then reach up to rap at the windowpane. The noise jump-started Larry's heart and he walked to the door and looked through the glass. He yanked the door open.

"Yes?" He demanded and the figure there stepped back in surprise.

"Oh, hello, sir, I'm sorry to disturb you..."

"What do you want?"

"I'm just... well ..." The young man in the suit coat and tie thrust two small magazines in Larry's direction. Larry took them without looking. "I want to give you some literature because in these trying times, we all need something to..." The nervous speech sounded rehearsed and was delivered rapid-fire. Larry relaxed his hand on the door and glanced at the magazines. "...we need something to cling to, to believe in, and..."

"I was in the middle of something," Larry said. "You'll have to excuse me."

"I'm sorry, sir." The young man backed down the steps. "I'll just leave you those magazines."

"Thank you." Larry started to close the door.

"Your mailbox is full," the young man said and turned his back, tramping across the lawn to the house next door.

My mailbox is full? Larry looked to the side of the house. The bronze box there was plugged, more mail piled on the step underneath. Larry collected it all and closed the door. He fanned the mail out on the living room rug and, as he did in his own home, separated the junk from the bills and the personal. Every piece of mail was addressed to Larry Hansen and none of it was very personal.

Larry took the bills back to the bedroom-slash-office. The man's finances were not hard to figure out. He had a simple life. Larry sat at the desk. Wouldn't this guy go paperless? Larry glanced up at the computer screen. Whatever the other Larry had been working on was still flashing there. It was a long paragraph that the other Larry had not responded to yet. It was a letter from a man who called himself Paul. He was dissatisfied with his home life; his daughter did not respect him, and he barely spoke to his wife anymore. Paul was having difficulty at work. His boss did not respect him, and he was not sure why he even still worked where he worked. There was a guy at work named Warren who was a loser drunk but for some reason got along better than he did. Paul was bullied by a snob named Lisa. The letter was long, and the salutation read: "Please help me. Paul."

Larry sat stunned at the coincidence. At all the signs, really, that were boxing him around the ears today. It was like his way out; everything was pointing to his escape. He leaned back and the chair complained under his weight. He reached for the keyboard. "Sounds like you need a vacation..." He began to type. No. Paul's problem sounded more intricate than simple stress. It required more thought. He pressed the backspace key until the words disappeared. He second guessed himself and typed the line again. Would they be able to set up an online interview soon? And like another sign, he received a message within minutes. Yes, that would be great, Paul had typed back.

Larry sat in the office and glanced around the room. No pictures on the walls and the bed was unmade. There was a bookshelf and Larry wondered if they had the same taste in novels. He decided to get up and check the kitchen for something to eat.

Chapter 9: Lisa

Lisa knew that this gangly beanpole was not a missing person. She looked right at his face over the perfume aisle, and he looked right into her eyes. His face had gone red and he skedaddled out of there. There was no question it was him. There was also no question that he watched her slip the useless perfume and cologne bottles into her purse. How long had he been watching her and how much did he see? What the hell was he doing there? She could not tell Bryce she had seen him; Bryce would call the police. And the police would call her. Where did you see him? At the mall. Which section? The fragrance section. Thank you, Mrs. Mayor, we will check the surveillance cameras. Fuck that, you will, she thought. It would be a black eye on her husband's upcoming election and on her marriage. There was no way she could explain it away. The attempted alcoholism, yes. The attempted affair, which he may or may not have believed, yes. But if his constituents knew the mayor's wife was a shoplifter, it would ruin his career. It would be a scandal that would cost him an election. Sure, she loved their lifestyle, but they would make do. She loved him. She could not destroy him like that. She would rather see that useless prick Larry Hansen dead than to embarrass her husband in such a way.

Further, she was not going to let Larry Hansen, of all people, destroy the one thing she found pleasure in. She could not explain why she was compelled to do what she did, or why it gave her a release, or some sense of escape or freedom. That did not matter. What mattered was, it was her thing. It did bring her joy in her otherwise shitty existence. Lisa would not let Larry Hansen take that from her. And why was he missing, anyway. Why had he not told his own wife where he was? Or even Bryce. Just up and gone. But not gone. That was him in the mall, one hundred percent. What was his deal? If you are trying to run away or disappear, why stay in the same city? He would have to stay somewhere, and surely his wife would have checked the credit cards and bank activity. He must have pulled a lot of cash from his account if he was hiding out in a hotel somewhere. But again, why?

She saw Paul when he came out of Bryce's office after talking to the two RCMPs. My, wasn't that one officer good looking? Paul, however, looked as though he had seen a ghost. His face was pale, and she had never seen his lips stand out so red against his face before. She followed him down the hall and into the elevator. He would not talk and would not look at her, either. His left leg was jittering as he stood, waiting to get to the ground floor. "What are you, going home?" Lisa asked and he nodded. "What are you, sick or something?"

"Yes, I'm sick," Paul said, and punched the elevator key to the ground floor again as if that would make the trip go any faster, or they would just magically appear in the lobby.

"You're sick a lot, Paul," Lisa said.

"I guess so."

Lisa reached a hand to the keypad and her finger hovered over the STOP button. "What the hell is going on, Paul? I have a right to know," she said, suddenly. Why she had a right to know, Lisa could not defend, but it seemed to work. Paul sighed deeply and leaned his back against the elevator wall.

"Can I trust you, Lisa?" he asked.

"Of course, you can," Lisa said, an exciting tingling in her stomach.

"No, I mean can I really trust you? With something very personal?"

"Paul, look at me." She faced him and held his shoulders, looking into his eyes. Like a puppy, he turned his face away to avoid her stare and she grabbed his chin and held it steady, so they were face to face. He could not avoid her steady gaze. "I am your friend; you can tell me anything," she said.

"Ok," he said finally. Poor little fucker, Lisa thought. He always was such an idiot.

The elevator let them out in the lobby, and they walked out of the office building onto Ballast Ave. Lisa guided Paul down the block to the pub the office sometimes frequented Friday nights after work. "What are you having?" Lisa asked Paul as they settled into a booth.

"I'll get a virgin Chi-Chi."

"What the fuck is a virgin Chi-Chi?" Lisa winced.

"A virgin Chi-Chi?" A waitress appeared at the table, young and pretty and smiling. Lisa hated her. "Do you want the usual cherry, as well?" The waitress had a friendly smile for Paul.

"Yes, please, Tina," Paul said. What the hell is wrong with this guy, Lisa wondered, and ordered a gin and tonic.

"Would you like lemon or lime?" The waitress asked.

"Neither thank you," Lisa said. "I don't think I'm in danger of getting scurvy anytime soon." Lisa stared down the waitress until the young woman's face flushed and she left to get their order. To Paul, she said, "What's going on? What's got you so upset?"

Paul's shoulders dropped and it looked as though he had shaken off a large hiking backpack. He folded his hands together and his eyes filled with tears. He rolled his head back and forth a few times and then stared at the table. "I don't know, Lisa. Sometimes I just don't feel well. I don't feel like getting out of bed in the morning, and the other day in the shower..."

"Yeah, yeah, yeah," Lisa said, waving her arm as if to dispel a displeasing odour. She had heard this shit before. Everyone had. It was the same story, over and over, and had been buffed into an office joke: do not, under any circumstance, ask Paul how he is doing. "I meant with the police," Lisa said. "With Bryce and the police just now."

"Oh, that," Paul said. He was pale again and his lips contrasted so red against his white face. Oh my God, Lisa thought, he is wearing lipstick.

The waitress came with their drinks. She placed Paul's gently down in front of him and put her hand on his shoulder. "You ok, today?" she asked. Please don't, Lisa thought, but he nodded and did not look up. The waitress set Lisa's drink down with a thud and stood expectantly.

"That will be a tab," Lisa glared and the waitress quickly walked away. To Paul, she said, "So tell me what happened. You looked pretty shook up. Let me be an ear for you, sweetie." Was the sweetie business a little too over the top? He seemed a little startled by it, but she watched him take a tentative sip of his little girlie drink and relax somewhat.

"They were asking questions about Larry," Paul said.

"What kind of questions?" Lisa asked. "And why you? They didn't talk to any of us."

"They don't think he is missing."

"Well, where is he, then?"

"Well, he is missing," Paul said. "But not missing missing."

It's like pulling teeth with this frigging guy, Lisa thought and swallowed half her drink. She motioned over to the snot of a waitress for another. "What does that mean, not missing missing?"

"He's gone. He hasn't spoken to his wife or been to work..."

"Well, I know that..."

"...but you know that," Paul said. "They know where he is, I think."

"Paul," Lisa leaned forward and attempted to take his hands in hers. He recoiled a little, but the waitress came with Lisa's drink, so she leaned back. The waitress gave Paul one of those 'is this person bothering you' looks. Lisa gritted her teeth. The insolence of these kids. Paul tried a smile and that seemed to satisfy the waitress and she left. "Paul," Lisa tried again, "work with me, here. You seem upset. What is going on? Be honest. You can trust me completely."

"They think I may have been in contact with Larry," Paul said finally, lowering his voice as though he were giving away the truth to a huge conspiracy.

Now Lisa was confused. "And have you?"

"No," Paul said. "I mean, yes. I guess I must have been."

She was ready to choke this melancholy, self-absorbed, little mopey bastard. "What do you mean by that? Paul, help me out here. I want to be a friend to you, but you're not telling me much. Have you seen Larry, or not? Do you know where he is?" Because I need to talk to him pronto, she thought.

"Lisa, I don't know what to do," Paul said and she could see the tears welling up again.

"What the? Paul! Did you kill him?" Now she was whispering. This revelation caught her off her guard. It had not even occurred to her. But then, why not? The police had questioned only Paul. There was a total paleness of his skin, besides his lips, when he left the interview. Could it be?

"What?" His voice went up an octave. "No! What?"

"I'm sorry, it's just that..."

"Why would you even think that? Do you think I'm capable of that? Lisa? Why would you even think I would even be capable of something like that?"

He was right, of course. Lisa knew in her heart of hearts that mopey little Paul was not capable of murder. It just hit her suddenly that maybe Larry was dead after all. And that maybe someone she knew may have killed him. And that she wasn't particularly sad or disturbed by that thought. But that didn't add up, either. He goes missing for, what, two week? Shows up in the department store. Then, so recently is killed? "I'm sorry, Paul," she said. "You just looked so stricken. The cops only talked to you. It's just... I'm sorry. I watch too many murder shows, I guess."

"Jeez Louise, Lisa," Paul said and slumped in his seat.

"I said I was sorry," Lisa said. "So, what is it then? What happened?"

"I accidently told Larry something that I have never told anyone. And would have never told anyone, especially some I knew. It's very bad. The worst."

"You did kill someone!" Lisa hissed.

"Lisa! Are you kidding me? I never killed anyone. Why do you keep saying that?"

"You said it was the worst thing."

"Well, not that bad. But bad. Bad for me, anyway, if anyone found out," Paul said.

"Well, whatever, that's your secret and I don't care." Oh, but she did care, now. She was dying to know this juicy little tidbit. She would have to pry it out of him sooner or later. "So how did you end up telling Larry? You met with him? After he went missing?" She used her fingers to make air quotes. "You both got drunk, and you told him your worst secret?"

"No," Paul said. "I was getting some counselling for mental health." He paused. Lisa knew he was waiting for her to say something like 'that's great' or 'you deserve happiness' or 'there is no shame and I'm immensely proud of you' or some stupid shit like that. But he was not going to get that from her. "Anyway," he continued, "I was paying for an online counselling session and I thought it was going fine. But something bothered me after the last session."

"And that was?"

"After I told this counsellor my deep secret, I told him I was afraid if people knew this about me; my wife, my friends, my daughter, my boss and you guys. Then this counsellor mentioned Bryce by name." A blank stare from Lisa. "I never told this person where I worked or what my boss's name was. He seemed to know me, though."

"So, you're saying this person was Larry? Why would you think that?"

"I didn't know it at the time," Paul said. "I had no idea who it was, but it freaked me out and I knew something weird was going on. I didn't want anyone to know my darkest secret."

He is dying to tell me, Lisa thought. Now that he let it out, he is dying to tell everyone. "So, when did you find out it was Larry? It was Larry, right? You know Larry isn't the best person to tell these kinds of things to. What kind of thing was it that you told him, Paul?"

"The cops told me they believed I was in contact with Larry. They showed me the URL address that I had been communicating with. That's how they found out it was Larry." Paul finished his drink and looked around the pub for the waitress. He was too meek to actually wave or call out and Lisa was damn sure she was not going to do it for him. He gave up. "I was talking to Larry the whole time."

"Wait, back up, Paul. I'm confused. Larry is an online therapist?" This was not making sense to Lisa.

"Larry Hansen is an online therapist. But our Larry Hansen is not."

"Huh?" Lisa squawked. So confusing.

"There are two Larry Hansen's. One Larry is a therapist who went missing a month ago, the other is our Larry who went missing two weeks ago."

"The cops are searching for two Larry Hansen's?"

"They are now, yes," Paul said. "When therapist Larry's online presence became active again after being, what ... dormant for three weeks, and then I was in contact with that account, they asked me questions. And I told them something strange happened when I told the therapist about my deepest secret. After I spoke with the cops, I knew it was our Larry."

"I'm not following," Lisa said. "So, our Larry has been talking with you online and he is pretending to be someone else. Who has the same name as he does?"

"I think so," Paul said. "I think that's what's going on."

"But why?"

"I have no idea. But Lisa..." This time Paul was the one to reach over and clasp her hand. "I am so scared. I can't let anyone know about this thing."

"What thing, Paul?" Lisa implored. Or implored as much as she was able.

"I can't tell you, Lisa." But she knows he wants to. He wants to so badly.

"Well, you didn't kill anyone," Lisa laughed. "Did you steal? Did you embezzle from Bryce?"

"No."

"Did you cheat on your wife?"

"Hell, no."

Twenty fucking questions here, you little virgin Chi Chi drinking... "Oh, Paul," she tried on her best motherly smile, "are you gay, honey? That is absolutely not the worst thing to be. It's going to be ok."

He paused a bit too long for Lisa to be convinced, but he said, "I'm not gay."

"Then tell me, sweetie."

Paul laughed a small snort of a laugh and dipped his head. He reached out to Lisa's hands again. "Oh, wow!" he said. "I used to think you were so mean. Such a bully in the office. You really care, don't you? Thank you, Lisa."

"Of course, I care, Paul." Such an idiot, this kid. And, what? A bully? Fuck him. But then it came clear. The lipstick. And when he lowered his head just then, she could clearly see through his shirt and tie, just the way it exposed a bit of his neck; there was a bra stop. Good grief. "It's all going to be ok, honey," she said and could not wait to tell her husband all about it later. But first... "So, do they know where Larry is now? Do You?"

"I don't, but they must. If he's being the therapist Larry they know where that other Larry lives."

"That dirty bastard," Lisa said.

"I know," Paul said. "I did not think he was that sort of person."

"Neither did I."

"Right? He was always so genuine and cool. He used to do this joke where he would tell me something was on my tie and when I would look down, he would sort of chuck me under my chin to trick me. It made me laugh."

"What a guy." Lisa tried not to gag. "There was something going on with him lately, though."

"What do you mean?"

"He shaved all his hair off. For no reason," Lisa said. "That's not normal."

"Well, yes. I understand a lot of that," Paul pouted. Right, Lisa thought, do not take the attention off your issues, Paul. He continued, "If he was depressed, as I am, then it makes total sense. And disappearing like that would make perfect sense, too. I can't tell you how many times I have thought of..."

"Sure, sure. I know." Lisa leaned forward, "This secret that you told Larry, does It have anything to do with the lipstick you're wearing?"

Paul covered his mouth with one hand and looked shocked. His face flushed. "What are you talking about? I'm not wearing lipstick," he mumbled through his fingers.

"Come on, Paul," Lisa smiled kindly. No mocking in her smile. Maybe on the inside, but not on her outward smile. "You smeared it when you covered your mouth. Are you a homosexual? It's nothing to be ashamed of."

"I'm not a homosexual, I love my wife. And I am not wearing lipstick."

"Well, you most certainly are wearing lipstick. A woman knows what lipstick is and how it is so expertly applied. You did a really fine job." Suddenly, Lisa sat back and exhaled in surprise. "Not gay, but... you like dressing up?"

"Lisa..."

"It's ok, Paul. I saw your bra strap. Nothing to be ashamed of. I am not the judging sort." Lisa could not wait to go home and tell her husband. They have not had a good laugh together in so long. "What colour panties?"

"I am not..."

"What colour, Paul?"

He dropped his head and said into the table, "Purple."

"Very good." Lisa smiled. The waitress appeared and asked how they were doing. "Bring us both another," Lisa told her.

"Not for me," Paul said. He was obviously flustered and was ready to leave.

"Bring me one, then, please." The waitress was still not liking Lisa very much and walked away without a word.

"I need to go," Paul said.

"I know you do, honey," Lisa patted his hands gently. "If it makes you feel any better, Larry knows something about me that I would really rather not let get out, too."

"Like what?" Wide eyed astonishment.

"Like I may have accidentally left a store without paying for something. I went back and paid, of course, but Larry doesn't know that part. It would not be good for my husband's career if it were known. They wouldn't spread the story that it was an accident, believe me."

Paul did believe her.

"I want you to talk to Larry again when you can. Online, or whatever. Let him know I want to meet him for lunch. Tell him I will give him five hundred dollars if he agrees to meet with me."

"Five hundred? Just for lunch?"

"Yes. And I will straighten him out about your little secret, too. There is no need for this to be all over the office, is there?"

"I will try," Paul said and stood up quickly. "I really have to go."

Lisa nodded and stood to hug him in a motherly way as the waitress brought her drink. "Thank you," Lisa said to her. "I will settle up just after this."

"You would really help me with this?" Paul asked and Lisa nodded. He hugged her again and hurried out of the pub.

Lisa sat for a moment and drank half her drink in a few sips. She stood and headed to the back of the pub to the washrooms. She washed her face in the sink and then opened the door to peer into the pub. Her waitress was busy at another table with her back to Lisa. She took a few tentative steps from the washroom and through the pub. No one was paying her any attention as she walked casually across the room, past her table, and out the glass doors to the street. She quickened her pace when she got to the sidewalk, her heart beating fast. A wild smile taking over her whole face, she felt a flush of pure...

"Ma'am? Excuse me! Ma'am?" It was the waitress, right on the street behind her. Lisa turned to face her, and the waitress held her bill in one slightly shaking hand. She has never had to do this before, and she is scared, Lisa thought. "You have not paid your bill!"

"Oh, my!" Lisa turned and held her hand to her mouth in mock astonishment. "Oh, I'm so embarrassed. Just so many things going on with my friend in there. He is under so much stress and I am so worried just thinking about him. This has never happened before. I am so embarrassed. How much do I owe you?"

"$34.33," The waitress said, confused instead of angry and scared now.

"Here." Lisa dug through her purse and found a hundred-dollar bill under three male roll-on deodorants she 'oopsed' from the pharmacy earlier. "You keep the change. And, again, I am so sorry."

"Keep the change?" Shocked. But Lisa knew this would appease her. She could tell by the cheap shoes the girl was wearing that this sort of tip would be very welcomed and put an end to any questions.

Lisa turned without another word and listened behind her to see if the girl would leave or pursue further. No. She must have turned and left. Good. That was a thrill. A cheap one and she had been caught, but still fun. She felt that tingle in her midsection and it seemed she did get a little wet.

Chapter 10: Ron

Ron felt he was overreacting over the two thousand dollars Warren had lost. It is true the idiot needed roughing up, and a smack from Jim and Lance was not a big deal, and the threat of something more may have been just that: a threat. Just enough to scare the dweeb into coming up with the money somehow or getting it back from the person he claimed stole it. That was not Ron's problem, that was Warren's problem. Still, they should not have strung up the old lady's cat in a tree. That was Jim's doing and, while Ron appreciated the initiative, harming an innocent animal seemed excessive. Really? He killed a cat?

It was not only two thousand dollars, though, was it? Warren could have turned that two thousand into eight thousand at least. After expenses, Warren's cut, Jim and Lance's allowance, that would have put three thousand in Ron's pocket. Not a lot, not big drug dealer money, but Ron did not aspire to be a big drug dealer. If Warren did this a few more times, and Lance and Jim kept their operation going, Ron and Stacey would have their house paid for in less than six months. This, without having to touch the inheritance money from Ron's parents' policy. The hustle money would never be enough to quit his machinist's job, but Ron did not want to do that anyway. This side hustle, as he called it, had put him through trade school and he enjoyed his regular job. Stacey enjoyed her job too, as ironic as it was, working with the RCMP. Ron made sure their regular lives were kept completely separate from the side hustle. They would retire early. The business with Jim and Lance was not his lifestyle, it was a way to escape to a better lifestyle later. Then, he would have nothing to do with it ever again. It was a pain in the ass dealing with Warren and Jim and Lance, and all the other half-wits and half-dangerous twerps he had to work with sometimes. He liked to stay out of it and let the others do the dirty work: the selling and the muscle stuff when necessary. The cat killing stuff may not have been necessary.

Ron would have to have a discussion with Jim about the cat. Jim was becoming increasingly erratic. When Lance called Ron earlier and suggested a meeting at Tim Horton's, Ron saw it as an opportunity to get things back into order. Lay out the mission statement again. Who were they? What were they trying to accomplish? What were they willing and able to do, and to not do.

Stacey had a soft spot for Lance in a way that only a woman who did not know what a dog he was could. She felt bad for Lance that he never found a serious relationship and was alone. Ron was never able to tell her that Lance had plenty of girlfriends at any given time, they were all just ten years younger than him. No one his own age would take Lance seriously because he was a basic man-child. He still worked as a cook at Shakey's pub, he still partied hard on the weekends trying to keep up with his younger girlfriends and their friends. Did he know how pathetic he must seem to them? His hair starting to turn grey, lines around his mouth, and bags beginning to form under his eyes. Many times Ron wished he could shake him and say: wise up, dude, you are in your mid-thirties. What do you talk about with those kids? But he could never bring himself to do that. In his own way, he felt sorry for Lance, as well. He and Lance and Jim were high school friends, and Lance had never made it past grade ten, literally and figuratively.

Ron slid into the booth and found an Ice-Cap waiting for him. Thoughtful. He nodded his thanks and took a sip. "Well?" he said. "What's going on?"

"I've got news," Lance said without a trace of a Mexican accent for once.

"What news?" Jim asked. He had his hands wrapped around his coffee cup and was staring at it as if it could walk away from him. In Ron's mind, Stacey should direct her sympathy to their friend Jim, and not Lance. But Ron knew Jim would never elicit sympathy; he was a large man, and quiet, not as charming, or funny as Lance could be. So, Stacey never warmed as much to Jim over the years. Jim had graduated with Ron, apprenticed as a machinist with Ron, and was best man at Ron and Stacey's wedding. He had been there when Stacey gave birth to twins. He was fiercely loyal to Ron, and Ron had introduced Jim to Penny, a girl from their neighborhood whom Jim married without a ceremony. It was one of Ron's regrets when it came to Jim. He wished he had not introduced them and wished he would have talked them out of getting married. Jim and Penny quietly watched Ron and Stacey's twins get older while they still tried for a child of their own. It was Jim who was unable to produce, the doctors said. Only Ron knew this. But then, Penny did get pregnant. And then, Penny was gone. Because Jim still could not father a child, and Penny moved to the east coast with a new, more potent partner. And still, only Ron knew the details. If Lance knew, he never once brought it up. Jim would never share things like that. Ron would not have believed it possible but, since it happened, Jim had become even more withdrawn. Perhaps this explained the cat situation. Maybe Ron would not bring that up in the Tim Horton's meeting. Maybe that was a more private conversation.

"Seriously," Ron said to Lance, "what news?" Lance was still smiling his dumb, proud smile.

"I found him," Lance said.

"Found who?"

"Larry Hansen." Lance could not hide his pride. "I found Larry Hansen."

"Cool," Jim mumbled into his coffee.

"Wait. Wait a second." Ron shook his head. "What are you talking about?"

"I mean I found that Larry Hansen fellow." Lance was all smiles.

"How the hell did you, Lance, find a guy that has been missing for, what? Two weeks?" Ron looked at Jim.

"More," Jim said.

Ron continued, "Missing for more than two weeks. No one knows where he is, and the cops have been looking for him. Everyone is looking for him and you? Lance? You found him?"

"Yeah, man!" Lance said, clearly not understanding Ron's nuance at all.

"Ok..." Ron held his hands out. "You want to tell me how?"

"Because he wasn't really missing," Lance said.

"Isn't that something," Jim mumbled. "He wasn't really missing."

"It was a mistake, he wasn't missing. He was gone, yeah, but he came back. I found him at the airport. He was just coming back," Lance said.

"So, not only did you find him," Ron was speaking slowly, "but you knew he would be at the airport. You knew when he would be returning?"

"Good job, Lance," Jim said.

"Thanks, Jimmy."

"Wait." Ron held his hands in the air. "Wait a fucking minute, here. Something is not adding up. How did you know he was going to be at the airport? Like, how did you know his plane was landing at that exact time?"

"Long story," Lance said and sipped at his steeped tea.

Ron craned his neck and looked around the Tim Horton's in mock astonishment. There were four old-timers in worn out caps huddled over their coffees in what looked to be a heated debate. A man in a suit was talking on his Bluetooth device attached to his ear and punching keys on a laptop. Otherwise, the place was empty. "You got some place to be, Jimmy?" Jim shook his head, no. "You in a rush to be somewhere, Lance?" Lance said no. "Then we have loads of time for this long story." Ron leaned forward and looked into Lance's eyes until the other man was forced to look away. "Don't hide nothing from me, Lance. You know better than that."

"Ok," Lance said, finally, "It was from Alice."

"Alice?"

"Alice."

"Who the fuck is Alice?" Ron said and Jim snickered until Ron glared him down. Jim looked away and slurped his drink.

"You know," Lance said, "Alice, Alice."

Suddenly, Ron did know who Alice was. She worked with Stacey at the detachment. When Stacey had suggested they host a company bar-b-q at their house a few months back, Ron had been wary and slightly amused. It would be mostly men and women from the administration pool, but there would be a few RCMP there, as well. Cops, Ron thought, in my house. It actually turned out to be a lot of fun. One or two of the cops even shared a joint with Ron in the garage. Lance crashed the party of course; the guy could smell a free meal from a mile away. Ron had taken him aside and hissed, "You know these are cops?" Lance told him to chill, he was cool. And he had been. Charming Lance, joking and telling stories, he soon had a crowd around him everywhere he went. That was his superpower and Ron had relaxed. Only now, sitting in Tim Horton's, staring at the dipshit himself, did Ron recall how much time one of Stacey's co-workers had been spending with Lance. How she laughed at everything he said, no matter how stupid or un-funny. How they had left together. How had he missed that? Alice. Dammit.

"We've been kind of seeing each other," Lance said.

"You met someone?" Jim said. "Good for you, man."

"Thanks, Jimmy."

"No, not good for fucking him, Jim," Ron spat. "Not good for you, Lance." Ron rarely raised his voice and he watched Jim and Lance flinch. It gave him no satisfaction and he felt a cold creep up the back of his neck. "How many times have I told you to keep Stacey out of our shit. She works with the fucking cops, you idiot. How many times?"

Ron stopped talking as the man in the suit gathered up his laptop and shuffled past where they were sitting. They watched his back as he walked out the door. All three glanced over at the old-timers still engrossed in their debate. They were far enough away to not overhear anything.

"It's no big deal, Ron, really," Lance started.

"No big deal?" Ron laughed humorlessly, "No big deal. Stacey loses her job? Maybe goes to jail? We all go to jail? What then? No big deal, he says."

"Calm down, Ron," Jim suddenly spoke, low and easy. It took Ron by surprise. Jim had never had the nerve to say anything to Ron before. He was Ron's fanboy. He carried out Ron's every order without question. His loyalty was something Ron counted on and did not take for granted. Where was this coming from? "Let him talk," Jim said and then turned to Lance. "You better explain this, man," He said.

"Seriously," Lance held out his hands in defence, "this is so not a big deal. We were just bullshitting, and I told her one of my friends works with that Larry Hansen guy that's missing. And she was, like, 'Oh, no, he's not missing. Everyone knows where he is, now.' And I'm like, 'What do you mean?' and she goes, 'It was a mistake, he took a few weeks off work, that was all, his boss got the dates mixed up or something' and that was it."

"Well, that wasn't it." Ron was whispering, now, his anger searing the table in front of them. "There is obviously more to it."

"Well, yeah. She told me he was coming in on a plane this morning and the cops wanted him to call once he was all settled in, just to clear things up."

"Ok, so, no problem," Jim said. "Now we know where he is, we can get the money back, Ron."

"For sure." Lance cheered up. "Problem, though. He's saying he doesn't know anyone named Warren and he doesn't know anything about any $2500."

"Maybe because it's $2000?" Jim offered.

"Wait," Ron said, frustrated beyond anything he had felt before. "You actually talked to him?"

"I did," Lance said. "I met him at the airport this morning. I held up a sign that said 'Larry Hansen' and he walked right up to me. Small, little guy."

"Are you out of your mind?" Ron asked.

"It's cool, man," Lance said. "No one saw me."

"Of course, someone saw you! You were standing in the middle of the airport with a sign with a missing person's name written on it."

"Only, he's not really missing," Jim said and Ron ignored this.

"Well, sure, maybe. No one would notice that, though," Lance said. "What I mean is, no one saw me put him in the trunk. He's just a small, little guy. It was no problem."

The cold on the back of Ron's neck intensified and turned to a dribble of sweat that ran down his back and made him shiver. "You... what?"

"What did you say?" Jim said, his mouth open. "He's in your trunk? Like, right this minute, in your trunk?"

"He's in your fucking trunk?" Ron shouted loud enough for the old-timers to stop talking and look over curiously. They stared openly and Ron lowered his voice. "Where are you parked, Lance?"

"Around back," Lance said. He had a look Ron recognized. Like a puppy who just now realized what a stupid thing it had done. Lance had probably thought he was going to get a pat on the back for this and now, judging from the reactions, knew he had made a mistake.

"Let's go," Ron said and did not wait for them as he left the booth and slammed through the Tim Horton's doors to the parking lot. He heard them following behind him and he quickened his pace out of spite.

"Open," Ron commanded when they got to the trunk of Lance's Malibu. Lance struggled with the key fob and finally released the trunk latch. It popped open too slowly and Ron grabbed the lip and opened it wide. Sure enough, Larry Hansen was a small, little guy and he was folded neatly in the trunk. He was wrapped in a green sleeping bag and his mouth was covered with duct tape. His hair was pasted to his forehead with sweat and he looked up at Ron with wide, frightened eyes. Ron slammed the trunk closed. "Holy shit," he said.

"I'm sorry!" Lance begged. "I just thought..."

"No, you didn't fucking think. You did not fucking think at all!" Ron shouted. There was a banging from inside the trunk. Larry Hansen was throwing his head against the metal. Ron grabbed the key fob from Lance and opened the trunk. Wide, frightened eyes. Sweat dripping from the prisoner. Ron reached in and slapped the man on the face. Not hard, but hard enough. "Don't," he said. "We are going to get you some water and let you out soon, so just shut up and we don't hurt you. Got it?" The man nodded and Ron slapped him again to make sure. He closed the trunk. "Get him some water," he growled at Lance.

"I forgot my wallet at home," Lance said.

Of course. "Fuck sakes." Ron reached for his wallet and gave Lance his debit card.

"What's the PIN?"

"Use the tap. Come on, man!"

Lance turned and jogged back toward the Tim Horton's entrance. He stopped and yelled back, "Can I get an Ice-Cap?"

"Holy fuck, Lance! Yes, get an Ice-Cap!" Ron shouted. Then thought. "Get one for Jim, too," he said.

"Thanks, Ron," Jim said.

"No problem." Ron leaned against the trunk and put his head in his hands, rubbing his receding hairline back and forth. "This is bad shit."

"Yup," Jim offered.

Ron yanked his phone from his pocket and punched the microphone button. "Call Warren," he ordered. He listened to it ring four times and then punched 'end call'. He texted: Answer your fucking phone or I am coming over there and burning your gramma's house down right fucking now. His phone rang immediately. The display showed Warren's profile.

"Jeez." Warren's voice sounded scared. "What the hell?"

"We've got Larry Hansen," Ron said into the phone.

"..."

"Hello?" Ron was not in the mood.

"I'm here. Ron. What do you mean you have Larry?"

"I mean we have your friend and we're bringing him over there right now."

"No! Ron, no!" Warren's voice was distorting, he was shouting. "My dad is driving in. He's going to be here in three hours. You can't be here."

"I don't give a fuck, you messed this up and we are going to be there in twenty minutes. Is that clear?"

"Yes," was the reply, and Ron disconnected.

Lance returned with a bottle of water and the Ice Caps. Ron stared down at the trunk. "Anyone looking?" Lance and Jim casually scanned the parking lot. It was virtually empty. "Ok," Ron said, and released the latch.

He ripped the duct tape from the prisoner's mouth. The man gasped and Ron held the water to his lips. He drank quickly, water spilling down the sides of his face. He took a few big gulps of air and said, "Listen, my name is Larry Hansen. I'm a nobody. I work at..."

"We know who you are," Ron said. "We are going to go see your buddy Warren and get this thing squared away. No one is going to hurt you. Just be cool in here and we're going to let you out in twenty minutes." Before the man could answer, Ron slammed the trunk shut. To Lance, he said, "Why do you have duct tape and a rope in your trunk?"

"For emergencies." Lance shrugged as if it were obvious.

"That's creepy," Jim said.

"It's not creepy!" Lance said as he walked to the driver's side of the Malibu. "Hey, Jim. It's not creepy."

Lance drove with Ron in the passenger seat and Jim in the back. The trunk was silent. "You know this is kidnapping, right?" Ron said.

"I guess I didn't really think things through," Lance said.

"Kidnapping, Lance. For two grand."

"Hey, Ron," Jim spoke up from the back seat. "The guy stole from drug dealers. I don't think he's going to the cops."

There was logic in that, Ron reluctantly conceded, and they rode quietly the rest of the way. As if Warren had been watching for them, the garage door opened as they pulled into the drive. Warren stood in the garage with his arms out in the universal body language signifying 'what the fuck', and Lance pulled the car inside, waiting until the garage door was closed before the three of them got out.

"What the hell, dudes?" Warren fretted. "My dad is going to be here in a few hours. Where the hell did you find Larry? What is going on?"

"This is all on you," Ron said and moved to the back of the car. "We want the money back and we will let him go. And after that, we are through with you. Understood?"

"Understood," Warren whispered. Ron could see the look of absolute stress and terror on Warren's face. And inside, Ron could relate. Kidnapping. For $2000. He had to stop working with these guys. As much as he loved them, they were losing their shit. Killing cats and kidnapping people.

Ron popped the trunk and Warren looked inside. The man in the trunk turned his sweaty face and frightened eyes to Warren and they stared at each other for a few seconds. "That's not Larry Hansen," Warren said.

Chapter 11: Paul

Paul sat in front of his laptop in his wife's bra and panties. It was midafternoon and his wife was at work and Carla was at school, so he was free to wear what he wanted and roam around the house with no care. He logged into the therapy website and typed: "Larry, I know it's you." And waited. After the last session he was not sure what to expect. And if Larry Hansen knew he was caught out, would he even respond? Then again, they were both sort of caught out, weren't they?

Paul woke after everyone had left the house and stayed in bed wondering about what he had just confessed to Larry, and now, Lisa as well. Then a weight had lifted off him and floated away. He did not care. He got out of bed and rummaged through the bathroom cabinets for a smoother razor than the ones he was accustomed to using. He shaved his legs carefully in the bath, vowing he would not be tempted to stay in for over a half hour ever again. He shaved his chest. The tricky and painful parts were under his arms. Shaving the arms themselves was easy. He wished he had long hair. He wondered how long it would take to grow out to shoulder length so he could at least put it up in a ponytail. Or style it in some way instead of waking up, showering and shampooing, putting gel in and running fingers through his hair and done. Five minutes. He pained to be able to sit at the vanity like his wife did and take that much care and attention and shape all that hair into something beautiful.

He had tried on his wife's bras before, but they were the practical ones, hard to fasten and bulky. He wanted to try something more fun. Sexy. He knew eventually he would have to buy his own, but he found some things she was fond of wearing when they had their date nights. He found a thong which was uncomfortable at first but strangely pleasing the more he walked around. The bra was padded a bit, so it was not bad, but he tried putting two oranges in to give the impression there were breasts, but that did not work so well, the fruit slid around and fell with the least bit of movement. Finally, he filled the bra with paper towel and, while it was not ideal, if he squinted his eyes in the mirror it nearly gave the right look. If he gained a lot of weight, would that give him breasts? It was not quite the body image he pictured for himself, though. He knew there were hormone shots or estrogen he could get that would make his breast grow. But he had just newly freed himself, was he really going that far at this early stage? The thought excited him enough to know that, yes, someday he would look into something like that.

He had not wanted to try on one of her dresses quite yet. He remembered their honeymoon and how she looked so sleek and sexy wearing just the lingerie and high heels. It drove him crazy that night, but not for the reasons she suspected, and not for the reasons he refused to let himself think. He found those same red heels in her closet, but his feet were too large, he had to wear them with their backs bent over the heel. Just not the same. He walked awkwardly around the kitchen and enjoyed the clicking sound they made. How did women wear these things? He almost twisted his ankle a few times but was soon able to strut steadily and walk with confidence. What pleased him most was when he relaxed on the couch and looked at his smooth, shapely legs with the shoes on. He extended his feet and moved them around, loving the visual. Fantastic.

His cell phone rang, and broke his obsessive wait for a reply on his computer. Bryce's face appeared on the screen. Not a chance. There was no way he was answering. He let it ring out and heard the notification that Bryce had left a voicemail. Too bad. He admired his smooth feet in the red heels posed daintily and got up from the computer desk and reclined again on the couch.

Bloop bloop. There was a text from Bryce. "Please call me now! It's important. It's about Larry." For fuck sakes. Paul reached for his phone and dialed Bryce's number.

"Are you sitting down?" Bryce asked excitedly.

"Ummm."

"They've found Larry Hansen," The Boss said. "Not our Larry, but the Larry you should have been talking to all this time." There was a pause. "How are you doing, by the way? Everything good?"

"I'm doing better," Paul said. "But I don't understand. They found the other Larry Hansen?"

"They did," Bryce said. "I'm not sure I understand all the details of it either, was he missing? Was there a misunderstanding? Did he try to run away?"

"I don't know."

"The point is, the thing that really matters, is if they know where Dr. Larry Hansen is, then that could only mean..."

"They know where our Larry Hansen is."

"...they know where our Larry Hansen is. Yes!" Bryce was almost shouting. "If you've been talking to Larry all this time, then that means..."

"He's taken over the other Larry's life somehow."

"...he's taken over... yes, that's it exactly," Bryce said, "and it could also mean that we know where our Larry is. He's in the other Larry's office or home or wherever that doctor does his business."

"Wow."

"Yes, wow!"

"But what does this mean? Why would our Larry just disappear and take over someone's life? It just doesn't seem like him. Something terrible must have happened recently."

There was a pause. "I have no idea," Bryce said softly. "I just want him back."

"I guess, yes. Sure, of course."

"And Marie does, too."

"Marie?"

Another pause. "Oh, his wife. Marie is his wife."

"Oh, right. How could I forget, I met her at the Charades party."

"Yes."

"Yes. You guessed that great clue about Def Leppard. Did you ever find out whose clue that was?" Paul remembered the amazement everyone felt that night.

"No, I barely remember it," Bryce said quickly. "I just want our office to get sorted and get back to normal as soon as possible. Are you taking your meds, Paul?"

Paul clicked the red high heels together sharply and the sound echoed off the high ceiling. "I sure am, Bryce," he said.

And after the call he sat in his high heels and lingerie and stared at the computer screen and waited for a reply. "I know it's you, Larry." He whispered the message as he typed it again.

He waited twenty minutes, and then: Hello, Paul.

Paul typed: What the hell?

There was a long pause, and then: I'm sorry, Paul. I really am.

Paul: Are you even a real doctor??

Larry: No, Paul. I'm nobody.

This rang eerily familiar to Paul, he rubbed his now silky-smooth legs together and paused before: You're not nobody, Larry. We miss you. Your wife is probably worried sick.

Larry: You don't know what you're talking about. I don't think she is.

Paul: Of course she is. She's your wife.

Larry: Maybe.

Paul: And Bryce is worried, too. He just called me.

Larry: (Laughing sideways emoticon with tears gushing from eyes) I'm sure.

Paul: I don't get it.

Larry: I had to escape. Things were not good. I used to be a hot shot insurance guy. I got burned out and I thought a low-pressure job any monkey could do would take the stress away. But things were still wrong.

Paul: A monkey? We have the same job.

Larry: I meant no offence. I saw a chance and I took it. Not very well planned.

Paul: No, It wasn't. They found the real Larry Hansen, I think. So they know where you are too, probably.

Long pause. Then: I see.

Paul: That's all you have to say?

Larry: The police will probably be over here soon then. Maybe today.

Paul: You have to talk to them.

Larry: Not yet.

Paul: Yes, yet. Like now. I will call.

Larry: Please, don't. Not yet. Let's talk for a bit.

Paul: And Lisa is desperate to talk with you, too.

Larry: Lisa?

Paul: Yes, she is so concerned. She offered you $500 just to talk. Imagine!

Larry: I know why Lisa wants to talk with me. I won't talk with her.

Paul: Why not?? What's going on??

Larry: Tell Lisa I know why she wants to talk with me and tell her not to worry.

Paul: I have to tell her something.

Larry: No, you don't. Don't trust Lisa with anything. She is not a good person.

Paul considered this. After a long pause: What do you mean?

Larry: I know why she wants to talk with me. I know something about her.

Paul: Like what?

Larry: I wouldn't tell you. The same way I wouldn't share what you confided.

Paul: Exactly! Thanks a lot, Larry! I thought I was in counselling.

Larry: Paul! I am your friend. There is nothing to be ashamed about.

Paul: Really? Really, Larry? I dress in women's clothing.

Larry: I knew you were unhappy somehow, some way. I could relate. When we started chatting and I got to know you better, I knew that we were the same.

Paul: Is that right? You dress in dresses, too?

Larry: No, that's just weird. But I knew you needed to escape who you were. Or just the stupid mundane existence of everyday life. So boring and crushing. Same thing, day after day with no end. And if dressing in women's clothing makes you happy, or gives you some sort of release, then why not? I didn't judge you. I was happy for you. The way you talked about it, I knew you had found a way out.

Paul: Yes. Thank you. I am starting to feel better.

Larry: And you can get over what others think. Your peace of mind is worth it.

Paul: Are you sure you're not a doctor? (smiley face emoticon)

Larry: LOL

Paul: So, what now?

Larry: I don't know, dude.

Paul: It's over, right?

Larry: Yup, it is.

Paul: Call your wife? The cops?

Larry: I seem to have created a mess with this. I need a day. Maybe two, if I can.

Paul: Can I come over?

Larry: No, I will see you soon. I am probably in trouble for being in this guy's house and taking over his practice like this. I'm sure this is not legal.

Paul: I will help you any way I can, Larry.

Larry: Thanks, pal.

Paul: No problem.

Larry: Can I ask you something?

Paul: Yes.

Larry: What are you wearing? (Wide eyes emoticon, laughing emoticon)

Paul: You're an asshole! (Laughing emoticon, rolling eyes emoticon)

Paul logged off and wandered around his house, getting used to the heels and the feel of the thong. He ran a bath with some Epson salts and used a luffa sponge on himself and finally understood what the thing was for. So good. He had a few hours before his wife and daughter would be home, but he changed anyway; he should be rid of any sense of femininity in the house before the real females came home. And then he paused. But I am a real female, he thought. And this was a further release. Something broke inside him like so many endorphins. This was it, this was

finally it. All his life. Was this why he could not talk sports with the guys at work? Was this why he did not enjoy it or think it funny when the other men fart in the elevator? Was this why he liked the look of his long, dark eyelashes, even at an early age? Or was this just a phase? How had Larry put it? An escape? Paul was not sure, but at the moment, right now, it did not matter. He felt liberated.

The strange thing was it had a lot to do with Larry. If he had not talked with Larry about the photo of Gordon Zanders and some of his own desires and feelings, he would not be feeling this elation right at this very moment. What a kind and gentle soul the man has. So understanding. Paul was so afraid of being ridiculed, but Larry listened and spoke with such insight and empathy.

And forgiving. Whatever Lisa wanted to talk with him about must be important for her to offer $500 just for a meeting. She would have been terribly worried about something. It was more than just a mishap at a shopping centre. Yet, Larry had said to pass on a message that she had nothing to worry about. What a gentleman.

It was a shame, now, the mess Larry was in. Granted, by his own actions, he did create it. But how could Paul just walk off into his new life while leaving the man who freed him be condemned? It did not feel right. Paul had simply wanted an escape, a fresh start. And that was all Larry wanted. Larry's desire, underneath all the differences, were the same as Paul's.

No. Paul felt compelled to help the man in any way he could. Would Larry need a lawyer? Most certainly. Did Paul know any lawyers? Most certainly not. Perhaps Paul's brother had a lawyer. But this was so convoluted he did not feel he had the energy to explain to anyone who did not know at least half the story.

Lisa.

Of course, Lisa. She was intimately involved in all of this. There was something already going on with her and Larry. Larry knew a secret about her that she did not want anyone to know. Larry graciously told Paul to let Lisa know that all was well. Once Lisa knew how Larry treated Paul's secret, she would be on Larry's side for sure. Larry had said not to trust her, but Paul had seen another side of her in the pub that perhaps Larry had never seen. Plus, Lisa was the mayor's wife, she would have connections. High powered connections. It could all be swept under the rug, so to speak. Paul could actually be useful in this. He had never felt better in his life. He imagined himself walking into the office in a sleek black dress, cut on the side, but not too far up. Black heels, but not too high. And a flowered blouse with no more cleavage than is appropriate for an office. Fully made-up hair, braided and flipped to one side. With no judgement from anyone. He would be the hero of the office. Larry would be fully positioned at work and, with counselling, functioning well. Lisa would become happier and attend more Charade get-togethers at Larry and Marie's home. This would all work out.

Paul found his phone and texted Lisa: "I know where Larry is! (smiley face emoticon)."

Chapter 12: Marie

In her life the last thing Marie thought she would do was have an affair. It was not in her nature and she hated the rumours and stories about friends, neighbors, co-workers and even family members who were caught out in affairs. To her it was despicable, and the meanest, most cruel thing you could do to your partner. How could anyone sleep with another man or woman, and then come home to their husband or wife, boyfriend, or girlfriend, and carry on as though nothing had happened. Kiss them goodnight, tell them you loved them. When you had just been with another person sharing an intimate part of yourself.

She never wanted to do that to Larry. She loved him. It was true that after so many years and with no children to occupy their time together and bind them, things had become a little stale. There were some bright moments, of course, but they were few and far between. It was just not something you walked away from. And she had no intention of leaving Larry for Bryce. It sounded cold, but practically speaking, her and Larry's house was paid for. They both had jobs. Larry had received a decent buyout from Consumer Life, and they could retire early and not worry. They were able to take trips twice a year. A divorce would be devastating and cripple them both financially. These things were never amicable, no matter what picture people tried to paint.

Besides, there was not even a consideration of leaving Larry for Bryce. Bryce was a mistake. A happy mistake, and one she was not quite ready to let go of yet, and she did want Bryce in her life forever now that they met. But she was not about to start a new life with him. She liked him a lot and perhaps she could even love him. She probably did love him. You could love two people, she discovered. It was not as though she was entirely unhappy with Larry. She was happy in her marriage. Bryce just seemed to be an addition to that. She had never connected to anyone the way she did with Bryce. The night of the Charade party where he guessed her obscure clue, they had locked eyes, and something just clicked. Like it had been there all the time. Like finding something you didn't even know you were looking for.

She did not know why, but she had texted him that night and the text and calls did not stop. It felt innocent, it was like they had known each other since they were twelve years old. He made her laugh. He made her feel smart in a way that Larry never did. Most of her married life she felt she deferred to Larry's opinions. But Bryce listened to her opinions on politics, religion, and music. More than a few times he told her that she may have changed his beliefs regarding certain topics. She knew she had made a real friend. He was a kind and generous man. He spoke so softly and warmly about the people in his office that, she knew from Larry, were probably idiots. Bryce had kind words for everyone. Warren was alcoholic, he wished he could help him. Jenny and Jeff were obviously in a hidden relationship, how terrible that must be. Lisa needs constant stimulation; can you imagine a life where you have everything, yet nothing makes you happy? What a lonely world. Paul seemed so disturbed, there was something he was hiding and, if he just let it out, he would be a happy man. Sure, Bryce sometimes had antiquated and almost misogynistic views of women in the workplace, and sure he was sometimes impatient with his employees despite his theoretical love for them, but he was a kind man. They never spoke about Larry. That was as taboo as the affair.

And Larry. No, she had never wanted to hurt Larry. Theirs was not a fairy book romance, nor was it a whirlwind. They both just sort of fell into it. She was not a popular girl in high school and university was no different. The boyfriends she had were boring and lifeless. Larry at least had a social life and people seemed to like him, though at first she could not see why. He threw amazing parties. Every party had to have a theme: dress like this, wear only this colour, things like that. It was a part of him that grated. His favourite joke was to point to someone's shirt or tie and ask: "What's that on your tie?" She could see the embarrassed and uncomfortable forced laughter of people when they were around Larry. She would be embarrassed for Larry, too. But he wasn't horrible. He was fun. It all just flowed into each next phase for Larry and Marie. Should we date? Sure. Should we move out of town? Nah. Should we get married? Why not? Should we buy this house now that Larry's Consumer Life career was taking off? Of course. Should we have kids? It was not a thing either of them were excited about, so, nah. It just went along that way. She had no complaints, and she was not unhappy. She was not looking for something outside her marriage. There were opportunities, sure. Men can be so forward even when they know you are married. No one interested her and it did not seem to be worth the hassle for a little bit of pleasure. She and Larry did not have a terrible sex life, so she did not feel she was missing out on anything. She was not lonely, either. What happened with Bryce was a mystery.

After their first texts she had felt strangely guilty. She had done nothing wrong, but it still felt wrong. Why would she be texting her husband's boss? Then she friended Bryce on Facebook and followed him on Instagram. Then came the usual liking and commenting on each other's posts. That feeling of a little excited ping in her stomach when his name would appear with a thumbs up on one of her pictures of her flower beds, or that she had just washed her car and now it rains, dammit. She knew something was happening that had never come close to happening before, but still it felt innocent.

Until the day she received the text at her flower shop. "Hi, it's Bryce! I'm in the neighborhood in about a half hour! How do you take your Timmie's?" He showed up exactly a half hour later with that huge, bright infectious smile and two double-doubles. They talked about everything and talking was so easy. There were never awkward moments of silence and no need to invent a topic to keep the conversation going, it just came so naturally. Again, there was no outward indication that something was happening. Yet, there was an electricity between them that she had never felt before. She knew if she were to reach out and touch him, there would be more than literal sparks, there would be lightning.

He brought her a cassette tape of Def Leppard's first album on that first meeting. "I found this in the attic," he smiled.

"Wow! That's from the stone age! Most of the kids that work here have probably never seen a tape." And they had a nice laugh over that.

When he left it was with a friendly "See you around," and "Let's keep in touch." Very nice. Very good. Very friend-like. Except that now she knew the truth of what was happening inside her. How her stomach flipped over when she watched him walk in the shop with the coffee. There was no denying it. It did not mean that one had to act on it, though. That was something different all together.

That night she went into her own attic and found the old Walkman and some headphones with the foam torn off. She played the old tape until it warbled and wrapped around the heads and finally broke. Oh, shit. She would replace it somehow. When she texted he returned with an LOL. Not to worry, he texted, no apology necessary.

She called him after a week of hundreds of texts. "I just happen to be in the neighborhood. Are you home?" She was indeed in the neighborhood, but she did not just happen to be there. She had planned either consciously or subconsciously to be on his street. She drove past his house and had seen his car, so she knew damn well he was home.

That was how it started, really. In his home. Did she know she was going to sleep with him that day? She could not be sure. But it was impossible to control when they were alone, the draw was so strong. So powerful. And the look of relief on his face when they finally lay down together was so obvious it made her want him more. There were only a handful of times after that.

Of course, she felt guilty. At the same time, it felt so good and right. They knew it was fleeting, though, he was not the sort of person to do this sort of thing, and she was certainly not. And she was the one cheating; the one with the most to lose. The unfortunate part was, as powerful and mutual as their attraction, so was the desire to be close friends. She wanted him in her life, she wanted to know him when they were eighty.

Ironic then, the day they were exposed, Bryce had come over to say goodbye. They would try to not even communicate for a while to see if this thing between them would fizzle and die. Perhaps then they could carry on as friends. Then of course, the thought of not seeing each other for who knows how long had fueled the desire and they fell into bed. They swore to each other it would be the last time. Second to last time. After the rushed first time, they had talked about their plan to separate and end this deceit, they had done it again, until, exhausted, they fell asleep.

Then they were caught.

If only she could explain to Larry. She loved him; she would never leave him. It was a thing she could not resist initially, but ultimately could. Their marriage meant more. But lately, Larry had been so depressed. He even cut off all his hair. He was so distant and was not letting her in. She felt despicable seeking affection with someone else, but it was over. She and Larry could get counselling, they could go on a trip, she was willing to do anything. The last time she heard his voice, he was in a hotel room. Then nothing. No money withdrawn from their accounts, no credit card use. Her mind did not want to go there, but it could only mean one thing. Larry was dead. Either by accident or suicide. She did not think he was the type, but she was not so naïve to deny what a devastating thing she had done, and how it could affect someone whose emotions had been precarious lately. It was probable that he was dead. It was her fault and she had not been to the flower shop in weeks, they could run the place without her. She did not leave her house, the guilt weighing so heavy. She sat in complete darkness and knew it was what she deserved.

So, her reaction should be forgivable or at least understood with empathy when Bryce called to say, "I think the police know where Larry is, and I think I do, too."

Marie sat stunned for a few seconds. Then, "That dirty, lying, inconsiderate, no good, selfish, sack of horseshit, fucked up belly-buttoned, cow-licked son of a bitch!" She began to hyperventilate. "How could he? I know I did wrong, but I don't deserve this. I thought he was dead! That fucking imbecilic, moronic, cross-eyed, odd-shaped ball, mother..."

"Marie, take a breath," Bryce said into the phone.

"What the hell is going on?" Marie was breathing rapidly. It was a full-on panic attack. "Where is he?"

"It's complicated," Bryce said. "I am trying to piece it all together myself, and the cops aren't saying much."

"I want to talk to the police," Marie said.

"I know," Bryce said, kindly. "I've asked them to meet with us."

"Us?" Marie was stunned. "No, no, no, Bryce. I don't want anyone to know about us."

"They don't have to," Bryce said. "I am an acquaintance of you both. I am coming as support, that's all. They don't have to know about us. Only Larry knows, and they haven't spoken to him, yet."

"Fine," Marie said. "That bastard."

"I'm picking you up. What are you wearing?"

"Are you joking? Bryce, now is not the time..."

"No!" He sounded panicked but laughed a little. "I mean are you dressed? Are you ready to leave now?"

He arrived within fifteen minutes and Marie was still fuming when she climbed in his car. "How could he do this?"

Bryce pulled into the street and eased along the avenue. "Put yourself in his shoes, Marie. What we did..."

"He made me think he was dead! I haven't been able to sleep or eat or run my business. I know what we did was wrong but be an adult. Divorce me! Don't disappear and make everyone think you were dead." She was yelling. "Imagine how I feel knowing I caused that!"

"I felt it, too."

"But I'm his wife!" Marie shouted and watched Bryce wince at her words. Poor man, she thought. Magically, in the same way it had appeared, the spark and flare between them was gone. For her, at any rate.

They arrived at the police station and were escorted to a stark interview room, the same sort Marie had seen on TV or Netflix a thousand times. These rooms are real, she marvelled fleetingly. They were offered coffee and then two men in suits came through the door, each with files in their hands which they placed on the table in front of Marie and Bryce, but out of reach. Even in her state, Marie was impressed with the taller one. He seemed to command the room. A handsome man, her mother would have said.

The good-looking office spoke first. "I am Detective Coxcomb and this is Detective Thorpe, we are working on your husband's case, Mrs. Hansen."

"Nice to meet you," Marie said and Bryce nodded to the two men.

"I know you have been through a lot. We have not spoken before, but it has become more complicated, and we hope to straighten this out, soon," Coxcomb said.

"For sure, the other officers working with us don't know a lot, but we are detectives. So, we got this. You better believe it," Thorpe said and Marie saw the good-looking officer give him a sharp look that made him sit back in his chair and purse his lips.

"We read through all the data and interviews, some of which we conducted ourselves," Coxcomb continued. "I don't feel we need to question you again about any of this, since we believe you had nothing to do with his disappearance. We think he is alive."

"I don't understand," Marie said. "Then where has he been? He hasn't used any money. He hasn't contacted anyone. No sign of him on Facebook, even. How could this happen?"

"What I'd like to start with," Coxcomb cleared his throat, "is why he would want to do this in the first place."

"We had an affair," Bryce suddenly blurted out, waving his hand between himself and Marie. For fuck sakes, Marie thought, he is just dying to tell everyone. She looked down and her face flushed.

"Is this true?" Coxcomb asked her.

"It's true," Marie said into her chest. Then she snapped her head up so suddenly her hair swooped back and around her shoulders. Something inside broke. Something dormant for so long. Something doormat for so long. Forty years of wallflower shifted off her back. No more. She was Marie Asmond before she was Marie fucking Hansen. She would not be pushed around any longer. She was a businesswoman and not unattractive for her age. She had above average intelligence and could beat any man she knew at a game of Scrabble. All the years of mentally abusive and belittling boyfriends and partners flashed in her mind until something hardened around her heart. No more. "And it was a mistake and I regret it. It happens. Have you ever had an affair?" She said this to both officers.

"No, I have not," Coxcomb said, levelly.

"Meh," Thorpe said.

"And that's why you're not married anymore, Thorpe." Coxcomb looked over at his partner.

"Oh thanks, Dave." Thorpe spread his arms wide, indicating the whole room. "In front of everyone? Really?"

"Look," Coxcomb said, back on track. "I just need to know the why of it. No judgment."

"Bullshit," Marie said. She could sense Bryce watching her. She knew this was a new side of her, for him. She was beginning to look forward to seeing Larry. There would be a look of surprise in his cross-eyes too, the bastard.

"No judgement," Coxcomb said again. "I am piecing together the why, I am going to get to the how."

"But you do know the how, don't you?" Bryce said meekly. Marie could tell he was trying to regain control. To be her knight. Too late. There were no knights for Marie any longer.

"It is your husband, and you have a right to know," Coxcomb sighed. "As strange as it sounds, knowing all we know about your husband, we believe he took the identity of a man with the same name. He could be working at an office downtown or at the victim's home now. We know the original missing person report was filed by mistake. The owner of the company Larry works for, not your husband Larry, the other Larry, made an error regarding a vacation schedule and reported him missing to his family and the police. Apparently, he is not close with his family or employer. This was cleared up relatively quickly. Then your Larry Hansen went missing. However, when there was business and internet activity on the doctor's website, we were able to contact Larry Hansen, the doctor, not your husband, and we were able to confirm that he was out of the country. We made the assumption, and the proper and logical one, mind you, that your Larry Hansen had somehow taken over Dr. Larry Hansen's practice."

There was a pause. "What the fuck are you talking about?" Marie said.

"I know, right?" Thorpe spoke up. "This is so fucked!"

"Thorpe!" Coxcomb said sharply. He took a deep breath. "We know that Larry Hansen is expected home today, and we are tracing the website to his home address. At this point he has really done nothing wrong, but we would like to speak with him in case your husband is indeed at his home. I would rather not have them run into one another unexpectedly."

"Tracing the address?" Marie asked. "You didn't just look in the phonebook?"

"Ummm..." Coxcomb said. His eyes shifted to Thorpe and the two men stared at each other, their eyes wide.

"Of course, we did," Thorpe said. "Pffftt.. " He stood up quickly and left the room.

"I think we have all we need here," Coxcomb said and stood as well. "Thank you." He shook Marie's hand and nodded to Bryce and left them both in the interview room.

Idiots, Marie thought. All men are idiots. "Do those cops know what you drive?" she said to Bryce, who sat with a dumb, confused look on his face. Typical. "Did they see you drive up in your car?"

"I don't think so," he stammered.

"Ok," Marie said. "Let's follow them."

From Bryce's car they watched the officers pull out of the lot and down the street. Traffic was slow so they were able to keep a safe distance while keeping an eye on all the turns Coxcomb was making. They followed them into the deep suburbs and parked at the end of one block when they saw Coxcomb's brake lights come on. He backed up the car and stopped. Marie watched the good-looking officer get out of the car and cross the street. She watched him banging on the front door of a simple, one storey yellow home. He pulled a business card from his pocket and wrote something on it. He placed it between the screen door and walked back to his car. But they did not seem to be going anywhere.

"Shit," Marie said. "Do you think that's where he is?"

"I don't know," Bryce said.

Of course you don't, Marie thought, I was talking to myself.

There was a small green sedan coming the opposite direction down the otherwise empty street, braking occasionally as if lost. It edged ahead and as it passed the officers parked car it sped up to the end of the block and turned the corner. As the car passed Marie and Bryce, the two occupants looked over in wide eyed disbelief, accelerated down the street and were gone.

"What the hell?" Bryce said, craning his neck to look after the green sedan that was now out of sight.

"What?"

"I think that was Paul and Lisa."

Chapter 13: Warren

He should have never gotten mixed up with those idiots. It looked good on paper and it was a good way to pay for his drinking, his meagre wage at his stupid job would not finance that, even if he was living relatively rent free with his grandmother. When he brought her rent, she would tell him, "Oh, sweetie, you paid me yesterday." And he would explain to her that, no, he did not, and she reluctantly took his word for it. Shameful, yes, but the last few months he had not paid, and she had not said anything about it at all. He was such a shit. But his drinking took on a greater significance in his life, pushing away friends and girlfriends and family, and the money became harder and harder to handle. How had he ended up like this? In high school it was fun, it was fun in college. Now the problems he used alcohol to escape from became the problems that alcohol created and needed escaping from by using alcohol. He felt trapped. When he took the $2000 worth of product and cash from Ron, he had full intentions of doing what was asked of him. He sold a bit locally and then suddenly the money was gone. He had painted himself into a corner. Two thousand dollars was not relatively a lot of money, but he did not have it. And Ron wanted it. Like, yesterday. He realized the gravity of the situation when they paid him a visit and smashed his grandmother's lamp. And killed her cat. Who kills a cat? They were serious this time, and he was scared.

His drunken, addled mind had not thought of the consequence of his lie. They had given him a way out. "Did someone steal it from you?" Yes. Yes, that is exactly what happened. Someone stole it. Who? Who did this? Well, let's see. A stranger? That would have required a huge story. It came to his mind too quickly and once it was spoken, it could not be unspoken. Larry Hansen. The guy was gone, for fuck sakes. Not even the cops could find him, and he left the country or was dead. Maybe Bryce and Larry's wife even did away with him. Warren did not care, he was the perfect scapegoat. He would never be found. The imbeciles he owed money to would not be able to track him down if the cops couldn't. They would never talk to Larry and find out the truth.

Except they did. And apparently, they had him and were coming over to his grandmother's house in less than twenty minutes. This was not good, and his father would be here soon. Did this call for the use of his grandmother's gun? That could turn bad quickly. Regardless, he searched her room and found it, loaded it, and hid it on top of the fridge. Please do not use this, he told himself. Only if things get incredibly ugly. And only to get them out of the house. No one is going to get shot.

Warren hobbled to the garage, struggling down the short steps on his crutches, and watched for them through the small glass in the garage door. He pressed the opener when he saw them approach. They pulled in and waited in the car until Warren had the garage door completely closed.

"What the hell, dudes?" Warren said as the three of them got out. "My dad is going to be here in a few hours! Where the hell did you find Larry? What's going on?"

"This is on you." Ron spoke first and moved to the back of the car. "We want the money back and we will let him go. And we are through with you. Understood?"

The way Ron spoke, so deep and low, made Warren freeze. He knew nothing he could say would make any difference now. He was in trouble. "Understood," he said, and Ron opened the trunk. Warren locked eyes with the man tied there with duct tape over his mouth. He was a tiny, little guy, easily folded into the trunk. Wide eyes and hair stuck to his forehead with sweat, stress, and worry. And Warren had no idea who he was.

"That's not Larry Hansen," Warren said.

"What?" Ron slammed the trunk on the pleading man and raised his arms in the air. "Are you fucking serious? What are you talking about? Who is it, then?"

"I don't know," Warren said. "I'm sorry, but I don't know what to tell you. That is not the guy from my office. That's not him."

"Lance?" Ron spun and grabbed Lance by his shirt. "What the fuck? Who is this?"

"It's Larry Hansen," Lance pleaded. "I have his driver's license. This is the guy that's missing. This is Larry fucking Hansen. Here, look!" Lance fumbled through his jacket pocket and pulled out a wallet. Ron released him so he could produce the license. Sure enough. Larry Hansen. Warren did not know where Larry lived, so he could not verify the address, but he could verify the man in the trunk was not the Larry Hansen he knew.

"I'm sorry, Ron," Warren said. "It's not him. Larry is tall and bald. Well, he's bald now. He shaved his head for some reason."

"What in the fuck," Ron said and yanked the key fob from Lance and opened the trunk. He ripped the duct tape from the prisoner's mouth, which sounded and looked painful to Warren. "Who the fuck are you?" Ron shouted at the helpless man.

"I'm nobody. My name is Larry Hansen. I don't know who you are, but if you let me go I promise not to..."

Ron slammed the trunk. "What the hell, Warren? This man is Larry Hansen. Are you jacking with me? I am not in the mood to be jacked with right now."

"I'm not jacking with you, Ron. Please," Warren said.

Ron jerked the driver's license out of Lance's hands and popped the trunk again. He held the license in the prisoner's face. "Is this you?" he demanded.

"Yes! Yes, I'm nobody," the man said. "Please!"

Ron slammed the trunk. He took three steps back and ran his hands through his hair. "Ok, ok," he said. "Let me think about this."

"This is too messed up," Jim said, and retreated to the corner of the garage. "What the hell, Lance?"

"Dude, that's him. That's Larry Hansen," Lance insisted.

"Except," Ron held two fists to the ceiling. "Warren says he isn't. We are fucked here, boys. What the hell is happening?"

"I have an idea," Lance said and gently lifted the key fob from Ron's clenched fist. He popped the trunk and stared down at the frightened man. "Hey, buddy," Lance tried to make his voice light and friendly. "We made a mistake here, ok? If we let you go, you won't do anything dumb like go to the cops or anything, right?"

"No, no, I promise. No one has to know. It was a mistake. I get it," the man said frantically.

Ron reached over and slammed the trunk. "Are you nuts?" he shouted at Lance. "The first thing this guy will do is go to the cops. Think!"

There was a banging on the inside of the trunk. Ron leaned against the car and groaned. The banging and yelling from inside got more insistent until Ron grabbed the fob from Lance and hit the release. "What?" he shouted at the prisoner.

"Can you please stop doing that?" the man shouted back. "Look, what do you want? If I have an answer, I will give it. But I am a nobody. I don't know what you want."

Warren looked at Ron and shrugged. Ron seemed to consider this and said, "Help me." Between the four of them they hoisted the man from the trunk and sat him down with his back leaning against the rear of the car. He was breathing heavily and would not lift his eyes from the cement garage floor. "Ok, who are you?" Ron said.

"I told you, I'm nobody. I am a doctor. My name is Larry Hansen. I don't know any of you and have no idea what you would want from me."

"It's really not him, Ron. This isn't the Larry Hansen that..." Warren swallowed hard. "...stole from me. Us. Stole from you."

"I didn't steal anything, I swear," the prisoner begged.

Ron walked to the garage door and with his back to all of them, said, "Call your girlfriend, Lance."

"Which one?" Lance said.

"Which one?" Ron spun around, his eyes flaring. "Alice! Alice! Who the fuck would I be talking about? Call her and find out what the fuck."

Lance fumbled frantically for his phone and dialed the number. "Hey! You picked up!" he said. "I'm good, just chillin'... nah... haha, ya right! ...I bet..." Ron rolled his hands over telling Lance to get to the point. "Listen, weirdest thing, you know that guy you were telling me about? ...No, that Larry Hansen guy ...well, it's really bugging me, because my friend works with him, I can't stop thinking about it ...oh? ...Really? ...You're kidding? ...And his wife was just there?" Lance looked up from his phone to the prisoner. He grimaced and mouthed the words, "I'm sorry." Into his phone, he said, "No, babe ...sorry, I just got a text from Ron. I'll call you later ...sure, that sounds good ...absolutely ...hey, can you bring that thing from last time? ...ya, that thing, haha ...No, seriously, it was awesome ...well, sure, but once I got used to it..." Ron slapped Lance on the back of his head. "Oh, sorry, babe, I have to go ...yup, you too, byeeee." Lance pressed end and smiled down at his phone. He sighed happily.

"Well?" Ron asked.

"She's awesome," Lance said. "I think this one is for real."

"Good for you," Jim said.

"Lance? I will break your frigging nose." Ron's teeth were clenched together. Warren could feel heat radiating from him. "What did she know?"

"It sounds weird, but there are two of them," Lance said.

"Two of them? What does that mean?"

"Two missing Larry Hansen's," Lance said, frowning. Warren could tell this was a lot for Lance's limited mental capacity to take in. "Alice was at work, she said that two detectives questioned Larry Hansen's wife and his boss. That guy is still missing but they think they know where he is. The other Larry Hansen...” He pointed at the prisoner seated and tied. “...was not missing at all. On vacation. Arriving at the airport this morning.”

“Whoah,” Jim said. “Trippy.”

“Yes! Yes, I told you. You have the wrong guy,” the bound Larry Hansen said. “I was out of the country. I don’t know you.”

“Alice also said the reason they may know where the real Larry Hansen is...”

“I am the real Larry Hansen!”

“...is because someone has hacked into your computer, pretending to be you. And probably cashing your pay cheques and paying your bills.” Lance said. And while Warren immediately put it together, he knew it would take Lance a while. Jim would never understand. But Warren knew Ron had pieced it together at the same time. Ron was quiet and listening.

“That’s why I had to cut my trip short,” one of the Larry Hansen’s said. “I forgot to shut the business down. Someone has been using my site, locked me right out. I do that sometimes. I forget to turn off the oven, I forget where I parked my car. It’s an issue I’m dealing with.”

“I do that, too,” Jim said. “How are you dealing with it?”

“I can refer you to a colleague, if you like?”

“Please.”

“Everyone shut up!” Ron shouted. “How could someone be cashing your cheques? And why would someone be paying your bills and taking over your business?”

“I don’t know.”

"I do," Warren said, and everyone turned to him. Everyone except Ron. Because Ron already knew as well, Warren thought. "Because Larry Hansen is not really missing, either. He is at your house right now."

"Exactly," Ron said.

"Wow," Jim whistled. "This is some whacked out shit."

"If those detectives already know this, then they are waiting to talk to him." Ron jabbed his thumb at the tied-up Larry Hansen. "And they know where the other Larry Hansen is."

"Ya, Ron, you better let me go over there and confront him." Warren said quickly. "He's going to deny stealing and you are way too wound up, it could get ugly."

"No fucking way, Warren," Ron said. "I am dealing with that. You are dealing with... this." He waved his hand around the garage, indicating the other Larry Hansen in the process.

"What the hell am I going to do?" Warren was in panic mode now. "My dad is going to be here in, like, soon!"

"Then you better hope that we are back in, like, soon," Ron said. He crouched so he was face to face with their prisoner. "You are staying here with this guy, got it?" He pointed at Warren. "We are going to get our money and come back. We are going to talk about letting you go, understood?" The man nodded. "No one is going to hurt you. Does this guy look like he could hurt you at all?" Again, Warren was singled out at finger point. The man shook his head. "Good," Ron said and stood.

"I can't just leave him here in the garage," Warren whined. "My dad will see him. What the fuck, Ron?"

"Where is your bedroom?" Ron asked.

"Upstairs," Warren said. "I use a room in the basement for computer stuff."

"Will your dad go down there?"

"I doubt it, but..."

"Take him down there, then," Ron said. "Tie him to a chair or something and duct tape his mouth. Be nice. And Warren? Give him something to eat and drink."

"And if my dad gets here before you get back?"

"Take your dad out to dinner and leave the backdoor unlocked. We'll come and get this guy."

"Fuck sakes."

"I told you, Warren," Ron said. "This is on you. So you are doing what you're told."

"Why can't you just put him back in the trunk and take him with you?" Warren was nearly in tears. The man on the ground shook his head back and forth, his eyes wide.

"This poor fucker has been in that trunk too long. He didn't do anything wrong," Ron snapped. "And what if we have to take that other schmuck somewhere to get the money? I don't want two missing Larry Hansen's in this car."

"This is so fucked," Warren whispered.

Jim and Lance lifted Larry Hansen by his arms and prodded him forward. The man cooperated and it was not difficult to get him down the basement steps. They put him in Warren's computer chair and secured him with two extension cords. Lance had to run back upstairs to retrieve the duct tape. "Can you please just let me breathe?" the man said. "I won't yell, no one would hear me. If his dad does come home, he can put the tape on me then. Please?"

160

They looked to Ron who nodded consent. "Thank you," Larry Hansen exhaled.

"Be good." Ron put his finger in Larry Hansen's face. Then he turned to Warren. "Get him some food."

"I will," Warren sulked. "Just hurry."

They left Warren and Larry Hansen alone, and Warren listened for the car backing out of the garage. He would not go up and close the garage door, he did not want to leave his prisoner alone for even a minute. Prisoner. How had this happened? He had to sober up and start making better decisions. Ron would find out soon enough that either the other Larry Hansen was lying about the money, or that Warren was. It would not take Ron long to figure it out, and Warren knew what the outcome would be. Ron had been so angry about the missing money; how would he react when he found out Warren had concocted a very huge story and gotten them all into this mess. Would Ron kill him? He was not sure. There was only one thing to do, he would tell his father everything. His father would disown him once and for all, that was certain, but his father would also take control. He would go to the police. Could Warren really do this to Ron? It did not seem like he had much of a choice. If Ron was willing to kidnap someone and even kill a small, defenseless animal, then there was no telling what his rage would cause him to do. Warren's life was over, either way.

"Can I please get something to eat?" the prisoner asked. "Or at least some water?"

Warren stared at his victim for a few seconds. "Fine," He said and went up to the main floor. He took a water bottle from the fridge and took it back down. He twisted off the cap and tipped it towards Larry's lips.

"No, wait," Larry said. "Just untie my hands, my legs are still tied. I'm not going anywhere."

"Screw that," Warren said, and tipped the bottle. Larry choked and sputtered the water all over Warren. "Watch it! Dammit."

"See?" the man gasped. "Just untie my hands."

"No," Warren said.

After a few seconds. "I'm hungry."

"Will you shut up! I am not in the mood," Warren spat.

"Your boss told you to feed me."

"He's not my boss. So shut up."

"Look," the man's voice firmed up. "I didn't do anything wrong, you idiots kidnapped me by mistake. Your boss said he was going to let me go, so I just have to wait it out. But it's been quite a day and I am fucking hungry."

"You!" Warren came right up to the man's face and breathed heavily. Slowly, he regained control. "You are getting microwaved popcorn and that's it. Got it?"

"Fine."

"Fine," Warren said. "Fucking rights, fine."

Warren limped upstairs and opened the popcorn packaging and placed the bag in the microwave. In three and half minutes he opened the popped bag and poured the contents in a plastic bowl. He took it back downstairs and placed it on the prisoner's lap.

"So, what? Are you going to feed it to me piece by piece?" the man asked.

"Hell no."

"Then how?"

Warren could see his point. He spun the computer chair roughly and began to untie Larry's hands. "This is sort of your fault, you know," Warren said, struggling with the knots.

"How is this my fault?" The man laughed. "How in the hell could this be my fault?"

"If you hadn't disappeared and caused all that confusion, Larry wouldn't have disappeared either."

"Oh, give me a break."

"Where the hell did you go, anyway?" Warren said, still struggling with the extension cords. Fuck Jim, why such intricate knots?

"None of your business."

"Hey!" Warren jerked the man's arms with the cord. "You're tied up in my basement. You will answer my questions."

"Fine." The man was getting a little too insolent as far as Warren was concerned. "I was overseas."

"Overseas? Just on a whim? You left that quick, and your boss didn't even know?"

"Something happened there suddenly." His voice got quiet. "There was someone there I had to meet. It was a small window of opportunity."

"Like a girl there?"

There was a pause. "Yes, a girl there. I had been talking with her for a while. They finally agreed that I could come see her. I was excited and I left in a hurry. That's how your prick friend got into my house. I left in a rush and left everything vulnerable."

"They who?"

"Excuse me?"

"You said you were talking to a girl for a while, and they decided you could meet. What the hell does that mean?"

"Dude, it's a fantasy. It's an escape that you can't get in this country."

Warren finally got the cords loose and watched Larry's hands fall limply to the side. "Are you talking children?" Warren asked the back of the man's head. "Hey!" he shouted and spun the chair to face him. The bowl fell on the floor, popcorn flying everywhere.

"Hey! The popcorn, man!" Larry said. "I am hungry!"

"Ok, wait," Warren said and limped back upstairs He opened a plastic popcorn bag and set the microwave for the popcorn setting. He stared at the oven's door for a second before realizing he had left Larry downstairs untied. He limped back down the basement stairs.

Larry was still sitting, tied at his ankles, sipping from the water bottle. "See?" he said. "I'm not going anywhere."

"Good. My friend isn't as nice as I am. He would kill you."

"I see."

"So, let's talk, Larry," Warren said. "Are you talking children."

The man looked down. "Not exactly children, no. But not something that would be good here in this country."

"Oh, dude!" Warren winced. "So, you took off in a hurry because, what? One of these children you paid for became available?"

"It's not like that," Larry insisted. "it's a different culture there, it's more acceptable..."

Warren slapped the man hard. His head rocked to the side and Warren could see the red imprint of his hand on the side of the man's face. "You're a fucking pervert, you fucking pervert!"

"Please, you don't understand, it's..." Suddenly, Larry went quiet. He tilted his head to one side and sniffed at the air. "Is something burning?"

Warren paused and smelled the room. Just then the smoke alarm let off a shrill and insistent cry that made both men jump. "Oh, shit!" Warren said. "The popcorn!"

Warren struggled up to the kitchen as fast as his boot would allow and opened the microwave door. Smoke escaped and he coughed. He

 grabbed the charred popcorn bag and batted into the air in the direction of the sink. It landed on the counter, spilling some of the black, crisp popcorn around the kitchen. He swatted the burnt bag into the sink. He grabbed one of his grandmother's dishtowels and waved it in front of the smoke detector in the ceiling until the shrieking stopped. "Holy, shit," he whispered. "What a day."

He walked back to the basement steps and opened the door. Halfway from the bottom, he stared into the startled face of Larry Hansen, creeping up the stairs. "Hey!" Warren shouted. "Get back down there, man!"

Larry roared and the sound was loud and primitive enough for Warren to stumble back. The man was rushing up the stairs toward him. "Hey! Don't, man! Whoah!" Larry was low to the stairs and hit Warren in the stomach, driving him back into the kitchen and onto the ledge of the kitchen island. The corner caught Warren in the spine and he shouted out in pain, his back muscles cramped and spasmed. Larry turned and struggled to find his footing to get out of the kitchen. Warren recovered as much as he could and grabbed the man around the waist from behind. He lifted Larry up and dropped him on his ass. Larry roared again and Warren was on him before he could move. He pinned the man down on the linoleum and the two lay there for a few seconds, breathing heavily.

"Cut it out, man," Warren said between gasps for air. "We are going to let you go. You didn't have to do this."

"You were going to let me go?" Larry's muffled voice came from the floor. "Don't be an asshole. There is no way you were going to let me go." He struggled a bit and Warren forced his weight down on him.

"Ron said we were going to let you go, and we will," Warren said. "Lance and Jim do everything Ron says."

"See!" Larry said. "You just told me their names! How would you let me go, now?"

"Well, hell, dude!" Warren said. "I didn't even realize I told you their names. You didn't have to tell me that, I wouldn't have even thought of it."

The man stopped struggling. "Yeah, that was dumb," He said quietly.

They stayed in that position, Warren considering the implications of telling Larry their names. He imagined Larry was contemplating the same. Stupid shit, Warren thought. "Ok, we can work this out. I am going to let you up... AHHHHHHH!!!"

Larry had wrenched his head free and found two of Warren's fingers near his mouth. There was an audible crunch as he bit down. Warren lifted his body off Larry and fell back to the floor in pain. His fingers throbbed and were too bloody for Warren to see the extent of the damage. "You prick!" he shouted. Larry stood up and spat red. Warren sat up and gripped the edge of the kitchen island so he could stand. He could not let the man get out the front door. There was no reasoning with the man, now. He had to get this back under control and let Ron figure something out. Warren was sick of this bullshit.

But Larry was not heading for the front door. He came around the side of the island opposite where Warren was just getting to his feet, his one hand hanging and dripping blood. Larry pulled the largest butcher knife from the wooden block on the counter. He raised it high and, with one of his signature roars, stepped quickly toward Warren.

Warren instinctively reached for the top of the fridge and found the handle of the gun he had hidden there. He pointed the gun at Larry and the man stood still, his hand still raised with the butcher knife. "Fuck off." Warren said. "Put it down."

The two men stared at each other, chests heaving. "You told me your friend would kill me if I tried to escape." Larry said, finally.

"That was..." Warren said. Had he actually said that? "That was a joke, man."

"A joke? What kind of a joke is that?"

"Well, I didn't want you going anywhere."

"Why?"

"Why?" Warren asked. That was a good question. If they were going to let him go, why not just let him go? "Because we have to figure all this shit out first."

"Bullshit."

"Not bullshit, Larry," Warren said. His hand throbbed but he had to talk to this guy. With his foot all booted up, he could hardly wrestle with the man for long. He motioned with the gun. "We're going back downstairs." He tried to sound menacing, but his hand was killing him, and he knocked the boot awkwardly against the island.

"No, we are not," Larry said.

"Yes, we are..." Before Warren could finish, Larry let out one of his roars and ran at Warren with the knife raised. His eyes were wide and crazed and he moved so quickly for a man who seemed so out of breath only moments before. Warren pulled the trigger, and the sound was loud in the confines of his grandmother's kitchen. He squeezed his eyes closed when he shot, and he heard Larry say, "ooof." And then everything was quiet. Warren opened his eyes and Larry was taking small, slow steps backwards. The knife fell from his hands and when his back came against the cupboard he slumped and slid to the floor. A large red stain was growing and billowing in the middle of his chest. His breathing was ragged and gurgling. His head fell to his shoulders.

"Oh, shit!" Warren whispered. "Oh, please, no!" He felt paralyzed. He watched Larry's chest heave up and down until there were two large convulsions and then nothing. Stillness.

Warren lowered himself to the floor on the opposite wall from Larry. He stared at the gun in his hand and set it down next to his boot. Slowly, the pain in his fingers came back. Blood was streaking every part of his grandmother's kitchen. He did not know how long he sat there before he heard a noise at the front door. "They're back," he thought. The door opened wide, filling the room with light and a dark figure stood in the doorframe. Whoever was standing there was bigger than Ron or Lance. Bigger than Jim, even.

"Warren?" his father said from above him. "What in the hell?"

Warren looked up at his dad. "Hey, pops." He tried to smile. "How was the drive?"

Chapter 14: Larry Hansen

He knew he could not keep this charade going much longer. He had been thinking of escaping for a long time, and it just seemed so perfect. But he had not really thought it through. People always knew him as the fun loving, party throwing Larry Hansen who was always playing hilarious practical jokes and was perpetually happy. But he was not that person. Not in high school, not in college, and not at Consumer Life where he made his career. He felt that any moment, any day, someone would realize he was faking. That he was a fraud. He was frightened of other people, truthfully. He never measured up and he never fit in. All those parties in high school and college were more or less a cover up. If anyone knew how scared and anxious he was all the time, they would pull away, and he would never have friends again. Only Marie knew what was going on inside him, and even she did not know all of it. She did not know about the suicide attempts in high school. She did not know he would disappear for whole weekends in college. She did not know that he would be both surprised and not surprised when he would return from these lost weekends, and none of his acquaintances knew he had been gone.

Seeking out Bryce for the job seemed like a way out, of sorts. He would still hold his gatherings, but he could tone it down a bit. He did not have to be 'on' all the time. Yet, the last few months working for Bryce had been going downhill. He started to feel those same feelings of inadequacy. He stopped having his socials. The last one was the Charades night. He hated himself and he did not know why. He wanted to be an entirely different person. He shaved his head to change his appearance, so that when he looked in the mirror, he would not be Larry. The happy accident involving a missing Larry Hansen was an opportunity he jumped at without considering the implications. Finding his wife in bed with Bryce was good timing.

He did not blame Bryce and he did not hate him. Sure, it was a betrayal, but Larry was able to empathize; Bryce was lonely. Larry had not known Bryce's wife, but he knew how devastated the man had been when she died. And so young to be a widower, how do you start over? Would you even want to? So, Larry understood the pull of someone's affection. He could even forgive Marie, after all, he had been checked out of their marriage for some time now. She must have been lonely as well. He knew her inside and out, and he knew with certainty that she would not enter into an affair easily or casually. It must have been difficult for her to even contemplate. During the affair she would have been torn up inside with guilt. He knew her. So, he did feel betrayed and belittled, but he understood. Was their marriage over? It could have survived an affair, hell, an affair had even crossed his mind over the years. But just disappearing on Marie? Without her knowing where he was or if he was even alive? Yes, this was unforgivable. Their marriage was over.

Was this a lesser worry? There were probably legal implications. Larry did not know a lot about the law, but he could not deny that he had committed identity theft and fraud. Would this mean jail time? A terrible fine to pay? He was not sure. The escape turned out to be ill-planned and potentially not an escape at all. He did not know how to be in prison. He did not imagine anyone would enjoy his Charade parties in jail.

He had wandered around the other Larry Hansen's house for how many days now? He only risked leaving for groceries and beer. And one time when he realized he did not have enough clothes for an extended disappearance. That was where he had seen Lisa. He watched her shoplift in the department store and that was why he did not duck out as soon as he spotted her; his brain was trying to process why a wealthy woman, the wife of the mayor, would be shoving cheap items into her purse. So, he stood watching her and she looked up into his eyes. They recognized each other and that was when he started to have doubts about the validity of his plan.

What plan? There was no plan. Stupid impulsivity is what it was. What if this other Larry Hansen turned up again, not dead after all. Just now the police had knocked on the door. He peeked through the bottom of the living room window and watched them walk to their car and they had been sitting there for the last ten minutes. Should he just walk out and give himself up? He knew he would have to eventually, they were on to something. If this other Larry Hansen were still missing, the police would find a legal way to enter the house and begin a proper investigation. They would find him there. It was odd that they hadn't already.

It was regrettable because the last two weeks had been bliss. He was able to just be himself, and sometimes he marvelled that he had not spoken out loud for the whole day. Beautiful. And the on-line stuff was fantastic. There were so many more fucked up people than he ever imagined. Most of the clients just needed to be heard and not judged. Some would thank him sincerely after a session. Larry did not have to be the practical joker or the life of the party, he just had to listen. Maybe he had missed his calling. He felt genuinely useful for the first time in his life, and he loathed to give it all up.

Larry sat on Larry's couch and hung his head. What to do? Well, he knew what to do, it was over. He would face whatever consequences there were. He was finished living the way he was living, anyway. If the police were still parked across the street, he would open the front door and talk to them, he would tell them everything. It would be a relief in some ways. He crawled on his knees to the living room window and again peaked under the curtains. They were still there. He took three deep breaths and resolved to do the right thing. But before he could, four things happened in succession that would make his decision for him.

The first thing that happened was, he recognized a car passing on the street, driving slowly past the unmarked police cruiser. He knew Bryce's car from the morning he saw it parked in his own driveway. And he would know his wife's hair anywhere. So, they had stayed together. He felt sick, it was truly over. Except she was staring directly at the house as they passed. He slumped below the windowsill. There was no way she would have seen him, but it was as though she was staring right at him, as if she knew he was peeking through, staring back at her. He dared another look, but Bryce's car had moved on and was gone around the corner.

This was the second thing: seeing his wife and Bryce together had rattled him, sure, but he was still determined to give himself over to the two police waiting in their car on the curb. Before he could get from his knees, he saw red and blue lights appear suddenly in the front grill and the back window of the unmarked police car. The siren made a 'whoop-whoop' that echoed off the other houses, and the car screeched from the curb, did a tight u-turn and, with squealing tires, was down the block and gone.

He felt frozen in position crouched behind the curtain. This was the third thing: he was staring at the empty spot where the police had been when he watched another car pull into the vacant spot. This car was too posh and expensive looking to belong in this neighborhood. He knew this car, as well. It had also been in his driveway on one occasion. He recognized the driver. Lisa. "What the hell?" he whispered, and he couldn't be sure, but was that Paul with her? They were talking and maybe even arguing, Paul was waving his arms around, very animated. It did not look like they were going anywhere soon. If Paul had been alone, Larry may have considered going outside and talking with him, after all, Paul knew what was happening. The charade was over, and Larry would have even asked Paul to accompany him to the police station for moral support. But Lisa was a different story. She knew he witnessed her shoplifting, there was no telling what her intentions were. She would not want it to go public. Not that he would ever expose her, but she did not know that. How had they found him? Probably the same way he had found Larry's residence, they looked it up in the phonebook. How had Lisa convinced Paul to bring her here? That was the real question.

Larry watched Lisa open the car door. "No, no, no." he whispered. He saw Paul shaking his finger at Lisa and she closed the car door. Larry considered his options. Should he just run out the back? Would he need anything? No, he was going to jail, anyway. He saw Lisa's car door open again, and then Paul's door open. They shut almost simultaneously. Paul was trying to convince her not to come to the house, or something. But Larry knew Lisa, and this was not a fight Paul was going to win. They would come to the door and they would start banging on the door. The neighbors would become curious and call the police. Larry was not going to talk with Lisa before he spoke with the police. He made up his mind to escape out the back; he would be in jail before Lisa had the chance to confront him.

Larry's knees cracked and ached as he stood, and he held the windowsill for support. When he turned around, the fourth thing happened that changed his plans about turning himself in. There were three men standing in the living room. Two taller men, one of whom was carrying a baseball bat, and a shorter man in the middle. "Hello, Larry," the one in the middle said.

"What the hell?" Larry tried to sound indignant. "Who are you? What the hell do you want?" His voice was not intimidating; it was shaking.

"You're a hard man to find, Larry," the one in the middle said, and the man holding the bat chuckled at this.

Larry held out his hands in appeal. "Listen, I don't know who you are, but I promise you I am not the man you are looking for."

"I promise you, you are, *ese,*" the other tall man said. Larry would not have pegged him as Latino. His hair was very red, and his face had that windswept look as though he had been raised in the wide-open spaces of farm country.

"No, I swear I'm not. I don't live here," Larry said.

"Are you Larry Hansen?" The one in the middle asked.

"Well, yes." This was going to be difficult, Larry thought. "But not the Larry you must be looking for. I can explain."

"Then you are the Larry we are looking for," The man in the middle said.

"How did you get in here?" Larry asked, he had been very careful to keep all the doors locked and the curtains drawn.

"Same way you did, *puta*, through the basement window you smashed," The Latino said.

So maybe he was the Larry they were looking for. But why? "Do I know you?" he asked, stupidly. Of course he did not know them, how could he? He would never be associated with a man who carried a baseball bat around. And he did not know a single Latino, he was certain of that.

"I don't think so. Maybe? My name is Ron," the man in the middle said, as if waiting for Larry to recognize the name. The man named Ron shrugged. "We have a mutual acquaintance that does some work for me occasionally."

"Ok, Ron, pleased to meet you," Larry said slowly, struggling to understand. He was not pleased to meet Ron. "We know the same person?"

"I am pretty sure you know who I'm talking about and why I am standing here talking to you," the man who called himself Ron said.

"Ron," Larry said, flatly. "I'm pretty sure I don't. I don't know what you want, and I can't even begin to think what I would have to do with you. Are you talking about Larry? Are you a client?" Had the other Larry pissed someone off with the wrong advice?

"Our friend, Warren, said you took something of mine," Ron said.

"Warren? From the office?" Oh, shit. "I know a Warren, yes, but what would I have taken from him that belongs to you?"

"Cut the shit," The one with the bat said and gripped the end with his large hands. This was not good.

"There is no shit to cut," Larry said.

"We want our $2500," the bat-man said.

"I thought it was $2000?" the Latino said.

"For our troubles," Ron interrupted. "We want our $2500. The $2000 you stole and another $500 for fucking us around. This has not been a great day."

"That's for sure," the bat-man said.

"I swear to you... Ron? I swear to you I have no idea what you're talking about. I did not steal any money. I don't know who you are. I know a Warren from work, and that's it, we are not really friends. I am a married man and I have a simple life. I am not one of you. I am not a criminal."

"You calling us liars, *ese*?" The Latino stepped forward and Larry stepped back toward the front door.

"No, I didn't mean that." Larry held his hands out. "I just would have no business being involved in... whatever business you're involved in. Whatever Warren told you, he is lying. He is a liar. Maybe not all the time, but about this he is a liar. He is a drunk and has zero work ethic. I don't trust him, I don't like him, and I like him even less if he has involved me in something I have no idea about."

Larry saw Ron's eyebrow twitch and there seemed to be a moment of doubt in his expression. Obviously, he knew Warren as well. Perhaps Larry would be able to talk his way out of this situation. Should he explain why he was Larry Hansen posing as Larry Hansen? These men had no doubt put it all together in the same way Lisa and Paul had. And Marie and Bryce, for that matter. They had all put it together at the same time, which was strange. But he doubted these men cared why he was here, and they would care less that he was going to turn himself in to the police. It probably would not help his chances if he were to bring up the RCMP, at this point.

"Ron?" the Latino asked. There was doubt there, too.

"Let me think," Ron said. But there was no time to think. There were three loud bangs on the front door right behind Larry.

It can't be the police, Larry thought, they would have identified themselves. Larry realized in the silence that followed that he had been holding his breath and he exhaled just as three more loud knocks startled him. "Larry!" He heard Lisa shouting on the other side of the door. "I know you're in there. Open this fucking door."

Larry held a finger to his lips imploring the intruders to be quiet. Ron did not look happy, and he whispered, "Are you expecting someone?" Larry shook his head and Lisa shouted again.

The bat-man nudged Larry aside and looked through the peephole. "It's two women," he whispered to Ron.

"Tell them to piss off," Ron hissed at Larry.

"I can't," Larry said. "Maybe they will just go away."

"We are not just going to go away." They heard Lisa shouting. "So, open this door and let us in."

Larry held his arms out in the universal body language for 'what the hell do I do?'

"Get rid of them."

"I can't open the door. They're not supposed to know I'm here. They are just guessing that I'm in here."

"I know you're in there," Lisa shouted. "I saw you peeking through the window."

"For fuck sakes," Larry whispered.

"Get rid of them," Ron said. "Don't screw around."

Ron and the Latino backed into the hall out of sight. The bat-man moved behind the door and gripped his weapon. Larry held the doorknob and breathed deep and exhaled the way he had been coaching Larry's on-line clients to do in times of stress. He opened the door slowly.

Paul was in a black dress with a pearl necklace that suited it very well. He had black heels, not too high, but good for an evening out where there would be dancing. He was wearing studded earrings that must have been clip-ons. Lisa was wearing a fake smile that was more of a grimace.

"Larry," Paul sighed. "I'm so happy you're safe. We were all so worried."

"Yes, Larry. So worried," Lisa said through her clenched smile. "Can we talk?"

"Lisa, I will talk with you." Larry was hoping to reason. "I know I have a lot of explaining to do, it's just, I can't talk right now. Can we meet tomorrow?"

"No, I think now is the perfect time," Lisa said and slammed her hand on the door. Larry felt the pressure there as he tried to keep her from opening it all the way.

"Lisa, this is strange, I know. You have nothing to worry about. I won't say anything."

"About what? This is just a misunderstanding," Paul tried.

"We are going to talk about that now," Lisa demanded and put her full weight against the door. She was surprisingly strong for an older woman, Larry thought, and before he could protest, they were all in the living room. The bat-man slowly closed the front door shut with the end of the bat and Lisa and Paul turned to face him. "Who the fuck are you?" Lisa said to him, confused and surprised.

The bat-man looked them both up and down and then said to Paul, "You're not a woman. Why did I think you were a woman? Why are you dressed like that?"

"I'm..." Paul stuttered. "I'm coming out?"

"Hey," the bat-man said. "Good for you.

Lisa stared at the man holding the bat for a few seconds. Larry could tell she was trying to process the situation. She really had no idea. Why couldn't she have just left? "Larry," She said, not taking her eyes off the man holding the bat. "I don't know who your friend is, but I would like to speak with you in private, if I may."

"Nah," Ron and the Latino came out from the hall. "I think we all need to just sit down for a minute."

Lisa's face went red. "And now who the fuck are you? I want a word with Larry, here. I would appreciate it if you all could just step out of the room for five frigging minutes."

The bat-man put the end of the bat against Lisa's chest and pushed her not so gently down onto the couch. She fell back with a grunt and a shocked expression. "He said let's all take a seat," the bat-man said.

Paul sat next to Lisa without being prompted and crossed his legs demurely at his ankles.

Chapter 15: Detective Coxcomb

"I really hate stakeouts," Detective Thorpe said from the passenger seat. "It's the worst part of this whole job. I wonder if there's a Timmie's close? I want a coffee. You want a coffee?"

"Thorpe, we've been here a whole two minutes." Detective Coxcomb exhaled. The worst part of the job was the stakeouts, he knew, but the worst part of stakeouts were stakeouts with Thorpe. There had been more than a few.

"I know, but who knows how long we'll be here," Thorpe said.

Coxcomb looked in the rear-view mirror and pushed a hand through his hair. He played with the front strands until he got the look he wanted. "Oh, Coxie," Thorpe laughed. "you're beautiful."

"Shut up," Coxcomb mumbled. "I know." He did not care that Thorpe caught him looking in the mirror, they had been together too long. They started as patrol and stayed together through every promotion, requesting each other. When the coveted detective promotion came up, it came with a stipulation from them both; they would work together. They were good together. Sure, Thorpe made his temperature rise and caused him to roll his eyes and shake his head often, but Thorpe was good at what he did, really. A little flaky and crass, but good intuition. At least he was never boring like the others he had worked with over the years, there was always a bit of drama in his life. Truthfully, Coxcomb appreciated it when Thorpe called him a narcissist in his joking way. At least he did it to his face and not behind his back in the gym or locker room like the others. So what if Coxcomb liked to spend a little more time on his hair and grooming than other men? Was it a crime to want to look good? No, it was not. Coxcomb had escaped the ridicule of middle school awkwardness where he had been ignored as an ugly duckling. He went through his winter and, as he got older, he blossomed in the spring. He could tell when women watched him. Men too, out of envy. Yes, he had escaped, and he was never going back, and he was proud of that. Only Thorpe understood, and for that Coxcomb considered him a good friend.

"You're really not buying this Hansen's story, are you?" Thorpe asked.

"Well, we haven't spoken to him, yet," Coxcomb said.

"Well, the whole thing... ya, he's missing... oh, wait, no he's not, he was on vacation and we forgot, but, oh, someone is using his computer and cashing his cheques..."

"I think he took off in a hurry," Coxcomb said, carefully choosing his words. Another thing Thorpe allowed him was the ability to think out loud, to piece things together as though he were actually running ideas past his partner. "I don't think it was a scheduled vacation. And I think something happened on that vacation to make him change his mind and come home in a hurry. Everyone involved seems to be embarrassed that they may have filed a false missing persons report."

"But that's not why we're at his house, is it?" Thorpe asked.

"Nope."

"We want the other Larry Hansen."

"Yes, we do," Coxcomb said. "The real Larry Hansen I could give a shit about. This other Hansen saw an opportunity and bailed on his wife. He took over someone's identity."

"But the affair?"

"Well, you were right about that, nothing new in an affair," Coxcomb admitted. "But to just disappear? Make his wife think he was dead? Cash other people's cheques?"

"But, Coxie, he came around to the station trying to straighten it all out," Thorpe said. "He presented himself and said he was not the missing man."

"He saw the opportunity after," Coxcomb reasoned. "Sneaky little bastard. Break and enter, fraud. So many crimes he thought he could just get away with?"

"So, you do think he's in there," Thorpe jerked a thumb to Larry Hansen's house. "That's why we're here. We're not waiting for Hansen to get off the plane and come home, we're waiting for the other Hansen to walk out the door."

"He won't answer the door, and we just can't barge in there. I know he's in that house. We have to wait for the real Hansen to come home."

"Which is the real Hansen? The fake doctor or the one pretending to be the fake doctor?" Thorpe laughed and Coxcomb had to admit it was a good point.

"Nice work on that background check on Hansen, by the way," Coxcomb said.

"Can you believe it?" Thorpe said. "Guy gets a two-year counselling diploma from community college and passes himself off as a doctor on-line. That's like one of those meter maids telling people he's a detective."

Thorpe looked sullenly out the passenger window. "We're the detectives," He said, more to himself than Coxcomb.

A car slowly passed them on the street and then picked up speed and was gone around the corner. Not fast enough to attract attention, but accelerating enough to get their attention. "Well, well," Coxcomb said, watching the car as it signalled and turned.

"Did you see that?" Thorpe said.

"I did." It was the fraudulent Larry Hansen's wife and her lover. "Interesting."

"They think he's in there, too."

"Yes, I think they do," Coxcomb said and smirked. It made his job in law enforcement so much easier knowing he could rely on the stupidity of other people.

"Isn't that something," Thorpe said. "Should we follow them? Talk to them again?"

"That's not a bad idea," Coxcomb said.

"Wow."

"What?"

"Thanks, Coxie," Thorpe said. "That's two compliments in a row. You never say shit like that to me."

What was he on about now? "I do all the time," Coxcomb said.

"No, you really don't," Thorpe said. "It's hard to get a compliment out of you, you know that? We've been together a long time, and you don't give out a lot of 'atta boys', you know?"

"Thorpe," Coxcomb sighed.

"No, it's ok. I know you're not that type of guy, but every once in a while, it's nice to hear."

"Look, Thorpe," Coxcomb turned in his seat, "I appreciate you as a detective, I think you have great work ethic. You're a smart cop and you're a Pitbull when it comes to cases. I wouldn't want to work with anyone else, ever. There. Is that good?"

"Well, not if I have to force it out of you," Thorpe pouted.

Coxcomb felt the familiar frustration when dealing with his partner, quickening of pulse, reddening of the face. Like a child, he was about to say, fine I take it back, when the radio emitted a sharp squawk. "Coxcomb?" It said.

"They never mention my name," Thorpe mumbled.

"Coxcomb here," he pressed the intercom.

"We have an incident here we want you to come have a look at," the radio voice crackled.

"Negative, I'm on surveillance."

"We," Thorpe said.

"What?" Coxcomb said.

"What?" the radio voice said.

"We are on surveillance, not just you. You always do that," Thorpe said. "See what I mean?"

"For fuck sakes," Coxcomb said.

"Hello?" the radio asked.

"Repeat, we are on surveillance," he said and looked over at Thorpe and whispered. "Happy?"

"Whatever." Thorpe looked out the opposite window.

"I think you're going to want to get over here," the radio said. "Sending the address now, it should link up. It's about your Larry Hansen fellow."

"Which one?" Thorpe spoke up. "The real one or the fake one?"

"I'm sorry?" the radio said.

"Hansen?" Coxcomb started the car. The address appeared on the computer and he pressed the route button on the navigation. "What's going on?"

"He's been shot," the radio said. "He broke into someone's house and they shot him. I think he's toast. We're here now."

"Holy shit!" Thorpe shouted and Coxcomb ignored him.

"Meet you there," Coxcomb said and turned on the emergency lights. He pulled away from the curb and spun the car around, tires squealing. They wove through the traffic with Thorpe letting out frightened squeaks when they took a corner too fast or as they passed a car that was not moving over quickly enough and came close to sideswiping them. "Cut it out," Coxcomb said over the siren.

"Your driving scares me."

"If I let you drive the bodies would already be at their funerals."

"Very funny," Thorpe said. "Look out! Fuck! What is the hurry anyway? The guy is dead, and the other guys are already processing."

This is true, Coxcomb thought. Still, speeding to a scene was a habit. Thorpe always complained about his driving. The navigation calmly informed them they were nearing their destination and Coxcomb could see two ambulances and four police cruisers along with an unmarked car similar to theirs.

"Is that Lee and Phil?" Thorpe asked.

"Looks like it, yup," Coxcomb answered and pulled up next to the unmarked cruiser.

There was yellow police tape strung up already and a few officers keeping the neighbors far enough away. One of the officers approached them as they ducked under the tape and walked across the lawn. "Good afternoon, detectives," He said.

"Greg, how you doing?" Coxcomb greeted him.

"Good," Greg said. "Weird. One of the paramedics said they were at this residence a bit ago. The guy we arrested had a broken leg or something trying to get a cat out of a tree."

"Shit, this dude has bad luck," Thorpe snickered.

"But the funny thing? The cat was strung up with a tiny little noose." The officer shaped his hands to signify a tiny little noose. "Someone hung it up there."

"That's fucked up," Thorpe said.

"No kidding."

"Did you ever get that thing on your arm looked at?" Thorpe asked.

"Ya, all cleared up." Officer Greg held out his bandaged arm. "It was a spider bite."

"No shit?" Thorpe said, and turned to the house. "Well, how does it look in there?"

"It's gross," Greg said. "Have fun."

The paramedics had already gone when Coxcomb and Thorpe entered the house. There was a photographer taking pictures and placards were placed on the floor in significant areas. The floor was slick with blood and a man was slumped against one of the kitchen counters. Coxcomb could tell he was dead. An officer stood guarding the front door and another officer at the door to which Coxcomb assumed was the basement. Apart from a lamp in the living room with a broken shade and no bulb, the house looked tidy enough, no sign of a ransack or robbery.

Two detectives were climbing up the basement steps, notepads out. "Lee. Phil," Coxcomb greeted them as they came into the kitchen.

"Hello, movie star," Lee said to Coxcomb. "What a mess, eh?"

"Lee!" Thorpe shouted. "And Phil Me Up Buttercup! My two least favourite detectives."

"Fuck off," Phil said.

"It is a mess," Coxcomb said, ignoring Thorpe and Phil. They had a feud. Something about who could bench press the most at the gym. They had a perpetually scheduled boxing match in the works between them. "They called you guys in for a break and enter? A self defence thingy?"

"You bet they did," Lee said. "Greg out there really has his shit together. He questioned the shooter, but when they found out who the victim was, his little spidey sense started to tingle."

"Ha!" Thorpe laughed. "That's funny! You know that thing on Greg's arm was from a spider bite, right?"

"Oh, shit. I never even put that together," Lee said. "That's funny."

"Not funny for him. Did you see that thing?"

"Oh ya. Disgusting."

Coxcomb was losing patience. "Thanks for calling me."

"Us," Thorpe said.

"Yes, us. Thanks for calling us. We were actually at a stakeout at this guy's house," Coxcomb pointed to the body on the floor.

"There's more, movie star, listen to this," Lee said. "When Greg calls for backup and gets the shooter and his dad into the cruiser..."

"There are two people involved?"

"No, dad came right after the shooting. That's who called it in," Lee said. "Anyway, Greg calls for backup and paramedics and then he starts to clear the house, and he finds a chair downstairs with extension cords wrapped all around it, like someone had been tied up. Duct tape, too. Popcorn all over the fucking place."

"Really."

"Ya, really," Lee said. "But the shooter didn't mention that he had been tied up, only that the guy broke in and came at him with a knife in the kitchen. And he shot him. That's all there was to his story."

"Why wouldn't he mention the intruder had tied him up?" Thorpe asked.

"Because we don't think he was tied up, dipshit. Can't you figure it out?" Phil sneered at Thorpe.

"Fuck you."

"Fuck you."

"Guys!" Coxcomb held out his hands to shut them up. "Do you think the dad is involved?"

"Nope, I don't," Lee said. "He only knows what his son told him. But the son is not saying much; acting really sketchy. I think there is more to his story."

"What's his name?"

"His name is Warren," Lee consulted his notepad. "Warren Parker."

"Holy crap!" Thorpe said. "Coxie, that's the guy we were going to interview the other day about Larry Hansen."

"Larry Hansen?" Lee was surprised. "There's the link. You already knew he had something going on with this Hansen guy?" Lee pointed to the corpse.

"Different Larry Hansen," Coxcomb said. "It's complicated. We'll compare notes once you're done here. Let's meet up tomorrow."

"Can we go talk to this Warren guy?" Thorpe asked. "Coxie, we should go talk to this Warren guy, right? Lee, you mind if we talk to this Warren guy?"

"Oh, be our guest, go ahead." Phil's tone was sarcastic. "Don't worry, we'll finish processing the scene and get you all our paperwork when we're done at two in the morning."

"That's enough, Phil," Lee said. Then to Coxcomb, "You should go talk to him. Sounds like this has more to do with you than us. The dad's lawyered up, but he's gone to a hotel. Kind of a loud mouthed, big shot. But you might get an interview with his kid before the lawyer can find out."

"Thanks," Coxcomb said. "You need a hand here?"

"Nah, we got it," Lee said. "We'll meet up tomorrow morning. You bring the coffee, though."

Lee and Coxcomb shook hands. Thorpe stared at Phil and raised his fists up in a boxing pose. "This Saturday? You ready?"

"I was born ready." Phil sneered at Thorpe. "But this Saturday doesn't work. Kid's birthday. Next Saturday. If you show up."

"Oh, I'll show up. You better show up."

"Oh, I'll show up. Be prepared to have your ass kicked," Phil said.

"Oh, it's on."

"It's on, all right. It's on like Donkey Kong."

"Who even says that, anymore, Phil Me Up Buttercup?" Thorpe said. "I said that when I was in, like, eighth grade."

"Which time, Thorpe? The first, second, or third time you were in eighth grade?"

"Fuck you."

"Fuck you, too. And by the way, you've been calling me that stupid name for months now. The song goes 'Build Me Up' not 'Phil Me Up.' You freaking dweeb."

"Whatever." Thorpe and Coxcomb left the house and walked across the yard. There were more neighbors than there were before, and another police cruiser showed up, playing blue and red light across the homes as the sun began to go down. Patrol men were taking notes and information from the on-lookers, but Coxcomb knew that they had not seen anything of use. He had spoken to bystanders on countless crimes over the years. Was he burning out on this career? He had been lied to more times than he remembered. His first instinct with every human being, even the grocery girl who rang his groceries through, was that they were lying to him. That they were hiding something. Maybe the two Larry's had a solid plan, after all. Escape seemed like a good idea, lately.

Coxcomb shook Greg's hand as they walked past. "Good work in there, you have a great future," he said.

"Thank you, detective." The officer seemed surprised by the praise.

Coxcomb and Thorpe got in their unmarked car and crawled slowly away from the curb, maneuvering through the growing crowd. They drove for five minutes in silence, which was unusual for Thorpe, Coxcomb thought. He always had a dozen theories that he would chat incessantly about, with Coxcomb only nodding and grunting affirmation. He was too quiet. "What's wrong, now?" he said patiently, as if to a child.

"Nothing," was the sullen reply.

"Thorpe."

"Well," Thorpe was looking out the opposite window at the houses coming in and out of view. "Did you know I was singing that song wrong to Phil all these months?"

Coxcomb looked over at his partner. "Well, yes. I thought you were doing it on purpose."

"I look like an idiot," Thorpe said softly. Coxcomb could not think of an appropriate response to this and the ride to the station was silent.

Coxcomb checked with the desk and was informed the suspect was waiting in interview room 6 with his lawyer. They brought in coffees for their guests and took seats opposite and introduced themselves. The lawyer was John Bangs and Coxcomb had had the pleasure before. He was not too bright but was a bulldog. He bulged from his suit in every direction and his tie sat vertical on his massive gut. It was hard to distinguish where his shoulders and neck began and his chin ended. His hair was thinning so badly that his combover stood straight up as if ashamed to be associated with the other follicles and was attempting an escape. He also breathed through his mouth, which Coxcomb hated and made him dislike the man more each time they met. He always got the impression that Bangs was meeting him for the first time. There was never a familiar greeting, just a perfunctory how do you do.

The shooter, Warren, was the complete opposite. Thin, pale, looking like he had not eaten in days. His ample hair was pasted to his head with what Coxcomb knew from experience was stress sweat. When Coxcomb saw this person at his workplace during the earlier interviews, the young man had seemed confident and arrogant. The person sitting in front of him now looked like a frightened teenager, or one of those drunks that had made a terrible mistake. Warren was shaking and could barely hold his coffee cup. Sure, he had just shot a man, but Coxcomb knew there was something more going on.

"Do you remember me?" Coxcomb began and from the corner of his eye caught a sharp look from Thorpe. His partner was already pouting, so he had to be delicate. "Do you remember us?" he corrected himself.

"I will be speaking on behalf of my client here, detective." The lawyer sat forward, exposing more of his belly than was previously hinted at.

"It's a simple question," Coxcomb said to the lawyer, and then turned to the suspect. "Do you remember us? Because we remember you." The suspect nodded. "You're Warren, right?"

"Yes," Warren said softly.

"We were scheduled to talk with you regarding a missing co-worker of yours, you remember?"

Coxcomb watched Warren turn his coffee cup around a few times. He pushed it away and laid his head down on the table. His shoulders heaved a few times, he was crying. The lawyer placed a meaty hand on Warren's back and scowled at Coxcomb. "That's all for today, if he is not being charged with anything, then I am taking him home," Bangs said.

"It's just curious, that's all." Coxcomb ignored Bangs. "The person we were going to question you about was named Larry Hansen. And the person who broke into your house was also named Larry Hansen. Such a strange coincidence."

"We are not answering any questions until I confer with my client alone. He has had a terrible day and I am demanding you release him so he can rest," the lawyer said, but Coxcomb saw his chins tremble with doubt. This piece of information had not been disclosed to him. Things were not as simple as they seemed. It was not just a case of self defense now. The man he shot may not have been simply an intruder; they were known to each other. As far as Coxcomb was concerned, Bangs did not need to know that the Larry Hansen lying dead in the morgue was a different Larry Hansen than the one Warren was about to start talking about. They could sort that out themselves and, when they did, maybe there would be answers for him, as well. Coxcomb was very confused.

"It was a mistake," Warren whispered from between his folded arms. He sniffled.

"Warren," Bangs said, more gently than Coxcomb had ever heard him speak. He had his hand on Warren's back like a father would. "You don't have to say anything. I'm here. I am going to take you to a hotel. Would you be alright staying with your father tonight?"

"They grabbed the wrong Larry Hansen," Warren sobbed. "No one was supposed to get hurt. We were going to let him go."

"Warren, enough" Bangs said sternly. "I am talking you out of here right now."

"No, I don't think you are," Coxcomb leveled a stare at Bangs. The big man went quiet, and Coxcomb knew he had him. "Sounds like kidnapping, and you know it. And someone was killed during that kidnapping, so that sounds like murder one, right?" Nothing.

"It wasn't my idea." Warren mumbled. "They brought him to my gramma's house. I had no idea what they were doing."

"Who is they?" Coxcomb asked.

"No more," Bangs suddenly commanded. "Charge him or I am taking him out of here."

"Fine," Thorpe spoke up, surprising everyone, not the least Coxcomb. "Stand up and turn around," He said to Warren and reached to his belt and produced his handcuffs.

"Detective!" Bangs stood and Warren turned his face to him, pleading.

"Shush, now," Thorpe said with more command in his voice than Coxcomb was used to. "Warren Parker, we are charging you with kidnapping, conspiracy to kidnap, and murder in the second degree. You will be detained in remand custody until a bail hearing. If no bail is made, then you will remain in remand until a trial is deemed necessary."

"Thorpe?" Coxcomb let his composure slip. "Can we talk about this?"

"Yes, you should talk to your partner," Bangs said. "Use your head, detective. His father is a powerful man. If you are making a mistake here," Bangs held up one chubby finger, "and I believe you are, then this will not bode well with your career."

"I don't even know what bode means." Thorpe sneered, and signalled to the two-way mirror. Two officers came through the door and led the snivelling Warren out of the room. Bangs stood huffing for a second and then stormed out himself.

Coxcomb turned to Thorpe. "What the hell?"

"Dude, we got him!" Thorpe was excited, a grin taking up his entire face.

"We got him, sure," Coxcomb said. "But he was about to break, there. Didn't you see it? Even Bangs was starting to fold, he was on the brink of telling us who kidnapped Hansen."

"Didn't matter," Thorpe said. "I already know."

"What?"

"Coxie, man, it's a funny story." Thorpe said and sat down at the interview table. Coxcomb stood for a bit longer than was comfortable or appropriate and finally gave up and sat down opposite. "I've been trying to nail this Alice girl in administration..."

"Good grief, Thorpe."

"No, listen," Thorpe implored. "She has a lady hard-on for law enforcement..."

"A lady what?" Coxcomb frowned. "Stop saying shit like that."

"Wait, listen," Thorpe said, growing more excited and animated. "So, Alice and I went for drinks a few times and she, like, really wants to escape her shitty job. She wants to be a cop. So, I'm humouring her. You know how it is when you want to..." Thorpe made a rude gesture with his hands and curled his lips in an obscene way.

"No, Thorpe, I really do not know how it is..."

"Listen!" Thorpe said. "So, she tells me about this guy she met at one of her co-worker's house, at a party or something. Like a low-level drug dealer, not someone we would be interested in. Maybe someone, but not us. And she is giving me some names and details. Nothing big, nothing that would make a dent in anything, you know? But one of the names she's dropping is this Warren dude." Thorpe indicates the door this Warren dude just left in handcuffs. "Honestly, I didn't place him until just now. I was just trying to get into her pants, you know?"

Coxcomb stared at Thorpe. "No."

"Well, whatever," Thorpe said. "I didn't put it together until we went to that office for the interviews. When she mentioned that Warren dude, she said this Latino guy she met was asking questions about the missing Larry Hansen."

"Which Larry?"

"No idea," Thorpe said. "But you and I are sitting outside Hansen's house and we get that call about one of the Larry Hansen's getting shot. When I see who the shooter is, it all fell into place."

"It did?"

"Well, no. But when this Warren dude said they kidnapped the wrong guy, it sort of did."

"I guess," Coxcomb said. Very confusing. Still, if Thorpe had the names of Warren's acquaintances, they could begin to unravel the knots. "You should not have involved a civilian, Thorpe."

Thorpe blinked and looked down at the table. "I wasn't... I didn't think she was going undercover, or anything. I was just humouring her. But then this came out and I thought, maybe..." He shuffled his feet under the table and blinked up at the ceiling. "I thought maybe you would be proud of me or something."

"What?" Coxcomb was taken aback.

"I know you always carried me along all these years." Coxcomb started to protest but Thorpe held up a hand. "It's true. You were always the hero, and I was always just the guy you brought along to the crime scenes. I never did nothing. Everyone knows it's you."

Coxcomb sat for a moment. "That's not true, Thorpe."

"It is."

"It is not. Why would I choose you If I didn't think you were smart and a good cop?"

"I don't know," Thorpe pouted.

"Give your head a shake," Coxcomb said. "All these years. You have no idea how much I value your instinct. And here we are. You just took this case ten steps forward."

"I did, didn't I?" Thorpe pumped up a bit.

"I am proud of you," Coxcomb said. "Very proud of you. And proud to call you my partner." Thorpe blushed. "You did a good job. I don't like that you got someone involved with a criminal, but I think your girlfriend gave you some great intel. I think you got this thing pretty much wrapped up."

"Well, I didn't ask her to get involved, she was already sort of involved," Thorpe said, and then paused. "She was... wow, she had to have been pretty close to this guy for him to give her all sorts of names and shit, right?"

"Maybe."

"Damn," Thorpe said. "Do you think Alice was sleeping with this Latino guy?"

“I don’t know, Thorpe.”

“Well, shit,” Thorpe said. “That sucks.”

Chapter 16: Ron

From an early age Ron had the ability to sense when something was wrong. He could tell his parents were in a fight before they even came home from an evening and relieved the sitter. He always knew when a teacher was about to turn up and was always the first to extinguish his cigarette and silently slip away while the others were caught. Small, intuitive things like that, and he felt it now. Granted, something was wrong; they had already kidnapped one person, and now three others were sitting on the couch. If it was not kidnapping, then it was unlawful detainment or some shit like that. Yes, this was wrong, but the feeling went beyond that. His instinct told him to move, and to move now. Screw the others, something was happening.

He had tried calling Warren. No answer. He texted: "I told you to always answer when I call." Nothing. Then a reply: "Where are you? At Hansen's? I'll come to you." How would Warren come to him when he had a guy tied up in his grandmother's basement? His dad must have come home, found the prisoner, and called the police. He texted back: "No, we left. BRB." They had to get out of there now. Would they leave the three captives? This was not worth $2000. Or $2500, for that matter.

"We gotta go," Ron said.

"What? Now?" Lance said. "What about the money this prick stole?"

"I didn't steal any money," Larry Hansen said. "Warren is lying to you."

This was a real possibility, Ron considered, but it did not matter. This was over. "Let's just cut our losses. All of you, just forget this ever happened. It was a mistake." He waved his hands over the trio on the couch. "This is not the Larry we are looking for."

"They just won't forget it," Jim mumbled, staring at the three.

"We can!" Paul spoke up, his mascara had run a bit with some frightened tears.

"We will," Larry said. "I want to forget everything. I want to go home. Paul?" He looked into Paul's heavily shadowed eyes, "I would have never said anything to anyone about you, it's your decision when and how you want to come out."

"Thank you, Larry." Paul bowed his head.

"And Lisa," Larry looked into her angry eyes. "Whatever happened in that store is your business. I know it would not look good for the mayor if they knew this stuff about his wife..."

"Wait. What?" Ron suddenly felt a chill. "We kidnapped the mayor's wife?"

The three captive's eyes went wide.

"No, no," Larry Hansen was saying. "No one has kidnapped anyone. We are all going to go our separate ways."

"Ron?" Lance said. His voice lost all the bravado Ron knew it for. Even Jim was looking to Ron for guidance. "This is the mayor's wife."

Before Ron could think of an answer there was a loud banging on the front door. This had to be the cops, he thought. An icy trace of sweat trickled down his back. He hoped Stacey and the kids would understand someday and not hate him.

"Larry, you dirty son of a bitch! Open this door! I know you're there; I saw you let Lisa and another woman in." Not the cops, Ron thought.

"It's my wife," Larry said, defeated.

"For fuck sakes," Ron said and motioned for Jim to let them in the door.

Jim opened the door to a surprised looking woman and grabbed her by the front of her blouse and yanked her inside, sending her spiralling and finally sprawling on the living room floor. The man with her stepped forward to protest and Jim butted his face with the end of the bat. Blood gushed from his nose and he made gurgling sounds as Jim pulled him into the house. Jim took a quick look outside to see if anyone was watching. Satisfied, he closed the door.

"Marie!" Larry Hansen started to stand. Jim used the end of the bloodied bat to gently ease him back down on the couch.

"Get a towel," Ron commanded Lance. Lance went to the kitchen and returned a second later and applied the towel to the man's broken nose. "We are fucked," Ron said.

"You broke my node!" the man said from under the towel which was turning red.

"Good, you bastard!" Larry Hansen shouted. "You're screwing my wife! You were my friend, Bryce!"

"It was an accident," Bryce said.

"What? You fell down and your penis landed inside her?"

"Hah!" Lance barked.

"Not cool, dude," Jim said to Bryce.

"How dare you say anything to Bryce," Marie roared. "I thought you were dead! You actually left and I thought you were dead. How could you do that to me?"

"Shut up, all of you," Ron shouted and the room fell silent. "I have to think."

"Ron, this is too much," Lance said. "Let's just go."

"We can't just go," Jim said. "We are not letting these people go. They know who we are." What did that mean? Ron looked at his long-time friend. There was something in his face, the way he was looking at their prisoner's. The way he had pulled that woman into the house and broken her lover's nose. Something was lost with Jim. He killed a cat. For the first time in their history together, Ron felt afraid of Jim.

The mayor's wife was looking at Ron steadily. The only one of the prisoners that was not either shaking or crying. "Can we talk in private?" She held Ron's gaze and he nodded. She stood and he followed her down the hall into the washroom. She closed the door. "You are all screwed," she said plainly.

"What the..."

"Listen to me," she said, and Ron held his tongue. "This is kidnapping. And your boys out there are morons."

"This is true."

"Hear me out. Let's say you let me go and I don't say anything." The mayor's wife continued, "Do you trust any of my idiot companions to not go to the police? And then the police will talk to me. What am I supposed to do?" She sighed and rested her bottom against the sink. She motioned for Ron to take a seat on the toilet. He closed the lid and sat. "You seem like the only one with your shit together," she said. "Do you have a family? Never mind. If you didn't you would have said so. So clearly you do and don't want to tell me."

"You're a smart lady," Ron said.

"I get by," The mayor's wife said. "Listen, I'm the wild card in this situation. If it was just my idiot friends out there, maybe you could consider just letting everyone go. But now you've kidnapped someone important, and that won't be swept under the rug. And your buddy with the bat out there knows it, too. You see the way he hit Bryce? He's gone off and he is not going to let us go." She paused to let Ron absorb this. "So, I want to make you a deal."

"Listen, lady..."

"No, you listen. My name is Lisa, not lady. And we are the two smartest people in this house right now. And we are both in a lot of trouble we didn't want."

Ron was quiet. He was in a situation with no good ending, and not because of his own mistakes. He would blame himself if it were right, but he would have done things differently, and now he was caught up in something bad. "Ok, Lisa. Fair. I am going to listen to what you have to say."

"Good boy," Lisa said. "I don't want to get hurt or killed and you don't want to go to jail, am I right?" Ron nodded mutely. "That's right. Your friend with the bat out there is going to hurt someone. As much as I despise those people, I don't want to see them hurt or killed, either. Don't look at me like that. This is a tight spot. Your friend could kill someone today, do you understand that?"

"Yes, I do."

"So, here's what we're going to do." She reached into her purse and searched the contents. Ron thought he saw a set of coasters that were on the coffee table earlier. She pulled out her cell phone and wallet and gave them to him. "There is a credit card in there with $30,000 available. I don't know if you can take it all out at once through an ATM and I don't care, that's your problem. I won't report it missing and I will confirm any suspicious withdrawals. Take what you can quickly and get the hell out of town."

"Ummm..."

"You could take it and kill us anyway, but I don't think..."

"...I don't want to kill anyone..."

"...that you want to kill anyone. Right. I know. This is for you, not your friends. You have a family."

"Yes, I understand," Ron said.

"So, now everyone is going to go for a ride. Take us out to..." Lisa thought for a second. "Take us out to Three Mile Bridge, no one goes out that way. You take our phones and our shoes, and you have a good three hours before any of us gets to a phone."

"Take your shoes?" Ron said. "And you walk back with no shoes?"

"Shut up," Lisa said and, to Ron's surprise, he shut up. "You take us out there and leave us. You take your family somewhere and be done with this. Or you go to jail for twenty years. Your choice."

"It's not even a question. I don't have to choose," Ron said.

"I didn't think so." Lisa smiled and slapped her thighs. "Boy! This is fun!"

"No, it's not fun," Ron said. "This has been too long. A couple more years and I was done with this and gone."

"You and those idiots?"

"No," Ron said. "The wife and I and the kids."

Lisa was smiling at him. "So, you do have a plan. I knew you were smart. I want you to call your wife. Do it now."

"I don't need to call..."

Lisa interrupted. "This is serious shit. Someone is going to die today and then you are up shit creek, buster. Make your plans and we all escape."

Ron considered this and waited for Lisa to break eye contact. She would not. Tough old girl, he thought. He liked her. He nodded and pulled out his phone and dialed his wife. It went to voicemail and he said, "I'm so sorry, sweetie, but it's plan C. Right now, today. Get the kids and meet me there. Take all the money from the green and red accounts, leave the yellow. We are not going to Spot A, it has to be Spot B, so do what you have to do and set that up. If I'm not there in four hours, don't wait, just go and I will contact you. I'm so sorry. I love you." He ended the call. "This sucks," he said to Lisa.

"I know," Lisa said. "Now, we go back out there. And shove me a bit to make it look real."

"Really?"

"Yes, really," Lisa stood and plucked a cologne bottle from the vanity and oopsed it into her purse. "Don't you dare judge me," She said to Ron.

"I didn't see a thing," Ron said.

They walked back to the living room with Ron shoving Lisa every step or two, saying, "Get going, get going" but not feeling convincing, even to himself. He sat her down on the couch next to the others.

"They are serious," Lisa said to her companions. "We have to do whatever they say."

"Here's what's going to happen," Ron said to the group. "We're taking everyone's phones." He motioned for Lance to collect them. Bryce wiped the blood from his phone and handed it over. Marie and Larry gave up their phones reluctantly and Paul reached in his blouse and produced his phone from his bra strap. Lance set the phones on an end table and went to the kitchen for a plastic bag to hold them. "Good," Ron said. "I am taking the phones."

"Now what?" Bryce asked through the towel. The blood had stopped but there was a lot of it.

"Who drove here? Whose cars am I dealing with?" Ron asked. Bryce, Lisa, and Lance raised their hands. "Put your hand down, Lance, I know you drove here, I was with you, for fuck sakes."

"Ok, ok!" Lance said defensively. "You don't have to get snippy, man."

"Dude, I'm sorry. Things are a little tense here right now."

"Are you going to kill us?" Paul asked. Everyone in the room looked to Paul, then back to Ron.

"If you all do what I tell you, no one is going to get hurt," Ron said. "I don't want to hurt anyone, but I don't want to go to jail, either. So, if it comes down to you or me, I will choose me. So, do what I say, and we will all get out of here in one piece and carry on with our lives."

"Someone already got hurt," Marie said, and put her hand on Bryce's shoulder. "You busted up his face.

You want to hit someone, hit this bastard. He's the reason every one of us is here right now." She was pointing at her husband.

"She's right, you know," Jim said and took a step toward Larry. He flinched. "Not one of us would be here if you hadn't decided to get a case of the fuckarounds. I should break your nose."

"No one's nose is going to get broken." Ron stepped in and put a hand on Jim's shoulders. He could feel the tension there, coiled and ready to spring.

"Except mine," Bryce said bitterly.

"Except yours, yes," Ron said. "But no one else's nose is going to get broken."

"Can we get to the plan, please?" Lisa urged. "You do have a plan, don't you?" She looked at Ron and cleared her throat loudly.

"Yes," he said. "Here's what's going to happen. We are going to drive you all out to Five Mile Bridge..."

"Three Mile Bridge," Lisa corrected.

"Right, I'm sorry," Ron said. "Three Mile Bridge. We are going to take your shoes..." He looked to Lisa who nodded imperceptibly. "And leave you there."

"Leave us? With no shoes?" Paul said, shocked.

"It makes sense," Lisa said. "No one goes out there anymore. By the time we get back to the city or a phone, these guys will be long gone. And we don't get hurt." She was speaking to Ron, but her eyes were on Jim. "Isn't that right?"

"That's right," Ron said. "Lance?"

"Ya, man, that's right. I don't want to hurt anybody. I just want this to be over, same as all of you. This has been one big mess."

Satisfied with Lance's answer, Ron looked over at Jim. "Jim?"

"Sure," Jim said quietly.

Was Ron really going to leave these people with Jim? He would have a talk with him before they left. Offer him something, threaten him, Ron did not know what. He was not the Jim he grew up with, the Jim he knew was a genuinely kind person. Where had this sullen anger come from? Of course, Ron thought. The affair. Jim had not taken his eyes off Bryce and Larry's wife. Jim was thinking about his own wife. Ron would make sure the three of them did not ride together.

"Boys," Lisa said. "I am going to reach inside my purse for a pen, is that ok?"

"No," Jim snapped. "I will get it." He reached in her purse and dug out a pen and a napkin and placed them in Lisa's lap. "Don't do anything stupid, I have a gun." He lifted his shirt to reveal the butt of a revolver sticking out from his pants.

"Holy shit, Jim!" Lance shouted. "Why do you have a gun? We don't need a gun!"

"Shut up," Jim said, and motioned to Lisa with the end of the bat. "Write what you need to write."

"I don't know if you will, but if you do," Lisa said as she wrote on the napkin, "in five hours, please contact this number and tell them where we are. Just in case we get lost, or something happens to us on the way." She passed the note to Ron.

Ron read the note: "The $30K is to buy your business. I will not take your jokers on; I will find my own. Send me your contacts and I will do the rest. This is fun." She provided her email address. Ron nodded. "I can do that for you, yes," He said.

"Thank you," Lisa said.

Ron knew they had to go now. He did not have time to contemplate Lisa's plan, he would do that later and it did not matter; he and his family would be gone. Guilt over Jim and Lance could come later. Who was more important? Stacey and the twins. Now it was just a matter of getting rid of everyone and getting lost. "Here's what we do. You and you," he pointed at Lisa and the small man in the dress, "You ride with Jim in one car. And you two," he pointed to the man with the broken nose and his lover, "you ride with Lance in your car. I am taking Lance's car with Hansen. Who knows where Three Mile Bridge is?"

"I do," Jim said, agitated. "But this doesn't feel right. Now they know our names."

Ron had not thought of that, things were moving too quickly, and his mind was already on the plane and flying away with his family. "Don't worry about it," He said unconvincingly. Even dim-witted Lance looked as though he had his doubts.

"Can we fit two people in the trunk?" Lance asked.

"No one has to ride in the trunk," Ron said. "No one is going to do anything dumb, right?" Everyone nodded and mumbled their assent. "This is almost over, but we have to go, like now."

Lance stepped out the front door and surveyed the neighborhood and empty street. The six of them walked to their designated cars. Ron took Larry out the back way to where they had parked Lance's car near a playground less than a block away. He started the car and drove around the block to join the rear of the convoy. Slowly, all three cars started down the avenue. Ron could not help feeling that any moment they would see the unmarked police car pull up behind them. The intuitive sense was screaming at him and it felt heavy. But he knew he had been right; this was almost over, and he would be gone soon.

"Are you going to kill us?" Larry Hansen asked as they left the suburbs and merged onto the three-lane main artery. "At this point, I don't even care. As long as it isn't torture, or anything."

"What the hell are you talking about?" Ron said, easing the car through traffic, following the lead cars through each lane change.

"I just want it to be quick, if you are."

"No one is killing anyone," Ron said, and then laughed. "Maybe your wife wants to kill you."

"Probably."

"Listen," Ron said. "I'm just a guy like you. I don't know what you've seen on TV and shit, but this drug business is just a means to an end, it's not even a huge operation. We don't go offing people left and right. I'm just trying to make a living. Just like you."

"I gave up on that," Larry Hansen said.

"What does that mean?"

"I gave up on all the money chasing. I had enough. It was pointless."

Ron stared over at his passenger. "It's not pointless. You make a living, you put shit away so you and your wife can have a good life for when you're older."

"Who cares?"

Ron sighed. They exited the three-lane and eased into the highway traffic. "You're just pissed that your wife is sleeping with your boss."

"I'm really not," Larry Hansen said. "I like Bryce. Better him than some shithead I don't know. He lost his wife, and he was lonely. I actually felt sort of happy for them."

"That's weird, man," Ron said. They drove in silence for a while and finally Ron could not help himself. "I'm just so curious, dude. What did you think you were doing? Did you steal from Warren?"

"No, I did not," Larry Hansen looked Ron in the eyes until Ron had to shift his gaze back to the highway.

"That little shit," Ron said.

"He has issues," Larry Hansen said. "He took your money thinking he would pay it back and things just got away from him. He probably used me as a scapegoat because I was already missing, and no one knew where I was."

"Yes, you were missing. What the hell were you going to do? Just live in that guy's house forever?"

"No one knew where he was, either. And we had the same name, so it seemed like a good idea at the time."

"And if he turned up again?" Ron asked. "Which he did, by the way."

"That didn't matter. I have money. I could leave right now and never see anyone again. They would stop looking for me after a while."

"So, why didn't you just leave, then?"

"I wasn't sure. It's a big thing to just leave your life and escape. Are you even allowed to?"

"Why not? You did it. Obviously, no one had to give you permission. Anyone, anywhere can just bugger off, if they want."

"As long as you can accept the fall out," Larry said. "In my case, I can accept the fall out. I don't care."

Ron's phone sounded a bloop. He shuffled around for it while keeping one hand on the wheel. It was a text from Stacey; the simple message had an emoticon of an airplane. They were at the airport. Good. So, this is it. Goodbye Canada, it's been great. This was happening a few years sooner than expected, but there you go. "What do you mean, fall out?" Ron had caught a chill at these words.

"I'm sorry?"

"You said, escape is easy if you can accept the fall out?"

"Oh!" Larry Hansen said. "This is not a conversation I was expecting to have." He laughed.

"Well, me neither, dude," Ron found himself laughing, too.

"Ok, for example," Larry said, and paused. "I am just thinking of people I know, now."

"Sure," Ron said. Damn, he was actually interested. The convoy ahead of them was slowing, leaving the highway, and merging onto another three-lane artery.

"Take our mutual friend, Warren," Larry continued. "He drinks, as you probably know. He hates his life. He wants to avoid all responsibility, but it will catch up with him as he gets older. He will lose jobs and relationships. He will be broke and alone. Was that worth it? Was his way of escaping worth it?"

"I don't know. I have never thought about it that way before." Ron was genuinely shocked. Ron sold drugs to people like Warren, he did not think about the people he dealt with. He felt a moment of confusion.

"And my friend, Paul," Larry went on, oblivious to Ron's moral crisis. "He wants so badly to be someone else, a woman in his case. Now, is he prepared to make that transition and welcome the alienation?"

"This is heavy, man," Ron said.

"It is heavy," Larry said. "While I was pretending to be Larry on-line, I realized there were so many hurt people out there. Just wanting to be noticed. Or just left alone to do what they chose without being judged. Or just looking for a way out of their boring existence. I could relate to them all."

Ron was quiet. The convoy changed lanes and merged onto a two-lane paved road. They must be getting close to Three Mile Bridge. "So, what was your plan?" Ron asked.

"I didn't have one," Larry laughed. "If the shit hit the fan, I always fantasized about going to the arctic."

"Hah!" Ron laughed. "The arctic?"

"No, not really. But some northern town out of the way, where people would get tired of looking for me. Be a bartender and just live in a room above the bar, or something. Forget all this pressure to be the right guy, be the right husband, be in the right career. Just serve drinks to the locals and be me. Me and free."

"Doesn't sound bad," Ron admitted. Where were they now? They had left the city limits and it would be dark in a few hours. He did not want to be doing this, he did not want to be with all these people. He wanted to be gone. The same as Larry, he supposed. Yet, soon, he would be gone, and Larry would have to face up to all he has done. It did not seem fair. "That's what you should have done, instead of all this," Ron said, finally.

"Yes, I should have," Larry said. "But it's too late. I'm in for fraud at the very least. I have to turn myself in. I'm going to jail. It's over."

"So, you have money to do this, if you wanted?" Ron asked.

"Do what?"

"Bugger off to Inuvik or wherever the hell you wanted to go."

Larry looked at Ron sideways and reluctantly nodded. Ron slowed the car until he could see the convoy ahead was out of sight. He pulled to the side of the road and put the car in park. He turned to Larry Hansen. "You have money now? Credit cards and shit? You have your ID and credit cards?"

Larry would not answer. Ron shoved him gently on the shoulder. "I do," Larry said. "Are you going to kill me?"

Ron sighed deeply and put the car in drive. He did a U-turn and started in the opposite direction. "No, jerkoff, I'm not going to kill you. We're going to the airport. You go your way, and I go mine. And I don't want to hear the name Larry Hansen again, understood?"

Larry Hansen understood.

Chapter 17: Paul

Paul saw in the side view mirror that the final car behind them had stopped. The car that had the leader of the gang and Larry. He did not see them turn around, only that they had parked on the side of the road. The middle car, the one with Bryce and Larry's wife and the other gang member, was still following. There was no chance they had not seen what Paul witnessed. They were being separated. These men were not going to let them go as promised, they were going to kill them.

The ride had been silent, with only Lisa speaking directions to the man that broke Bryce's nose. She was being kind and soothing, Paul could tell, trying not to anger the man. How could she be so calm? She had taken control, thankfully. Paul saw her in a new light after their time in the pub, almost like a mother figure. Loving and nurturing, but hard when she needed to be. Taking control. For the whole drive, Paul felt like crying, but he maintained composure to show her he was strong. But now that he knows they are going to kill him, why not fight? Why not scratch and scream and cry and bite? They were not going to make it out of this alive. The men knew this when they decided to kidnap the mayor's wife.

Paul also felt regret. He was finally free for the first time in... well, since ever. He felt now he could reveal his real self to his family. His talks with Larry and his brief confession to Lisa gave him that confidence. He felt brave enough to face them wearing the dress and the makeup. He felt strong enough to talk to his brother about it. If his brother could not understand, then so be it; he was who he was. Then he would have to talk with his wife and daughter, and that would be more difficult. He had no intention of breaking up his family, but if they decided they could not handle him the way he was, then he would find a way to work through it and carry on. He even felt he could dress this way at the office. Did he want to be a woman? He was not convinced. Probably. This would need discussing with someone more qualified than Larry.

But now it was too late, it was over. When his body was eventually discovered, it would be in his wife's sexy, yet subtle black dress. There would be so many questions and he would not be around to answer them or defend himself. He was not going to let this happen if he could help it. He glanced over at the man driving Lisa's car. He was a violent person, he had demonstrated that, but this man was not going to have an easy time getting rid of them all, if that was what he was anticipating. If Paul was going to die anyway, he was going to die fighting. The other's may want to fruitlessly beg for their lives, but he would not. He had gone too long hiding behind a suit and sometimes a shower curtain. He was not going to die with regrets like Gordon Zanders. When Lisa finally told the driver, "This road, right here, and we're at the bridge." Paul had made up his mind. When they found him, they would know that Paul fought to the very end. In heels, no less.

The gravel crunched beneath the tires as the car slowed in a cloud of dust. Paul heard the ticking of the resting engine and watched the other car pull up beside them. "Ok," the driver, the one who had broken Bryce's nose and was about to kill them, said, "this is it." Yes, Paul thought. This was it.

With one fluid, graceful motion, Paul pulled the door handle and opened the door, while the other hand grasped the keys from the ignition and pulled them out. Before the driver could turn his head, Paul was out of the car and running to the bridge only a few feet in front of where they were parked. He heard the driver shouting but he did not look back. He reached the centre of the narrow one-lane bridge and heard the river rushing over the rocks below him. It sounded a long way down. He lifted his arm over his head and threw the keys as hard as he could over the bridge railing and into the dimming sky. He did not hear a splash but knew the keys would never be found. They can kill us, but they will have to walk back to the city. He made it just a little more difficult for them. Paul turned and, as the driver rushed toward him, had the revelation that there were two cars, anyway. They could kill them and still drive back. He had not thought this through. Well, Paul thought, I tried.

"You little fucker!" The driver grabbed Paul by his dress straps and slammed a fist into Paul's forehead. Paul felt his ass hit the wooden boards of the old bridge. He floated for a while above everyone and hovered in the clouds, humming peacefully to himself. Years passed by. Then he was flung back to the ground in the present, listening to Lisa yelling.

"Leave him alone! Paul! What the hell are you doing?" He thinks it's Lisa. His mind was slowly clearing. Yes, it is Lisa.

"They are going to kill us." Paul thought he was shouting, but it sounded like a whisper to his ears.

"No one was killing anyone, you little shit." Paul felt himself lifted off the ground and shaken like a doll and tossed to the ground again.

"Jim!" Paul heard the driver of the other car, the Latino, shout. "Take it easy!" Bryce and Marie were shouting as well but he could not make out what they were saying. His ribs exploded suddenly from what was surely a violent kick to his side. Again, he felt himself lifted from the ground and carried backwards, one heel coming off and the other scraping against the surface of the bridge. Paul was pulled upward, and he could feel the bridge railing against his lower back, the man was holding him there and lifting him slightly. This is how it happens, Paul thought, he is going to throw me over. This is how I die. He heard the others shouting and pleading.

"You just had to fuck around, didn't you? You little shit," the man screamed into Paul's face. He smelled the man's breath and felt the man's tightening grip on the straps of his blouse.

"Fuck you," Paul managed, and tried to claw the man's face with the glued-on nails he found in his wife's drawer that morning. The nails came off without leaving a scratch.

"Got some spunk, you little shit?" the man said. "Good for you."

"Fuck you," Paul said again, he could not think of anything else. He spit in the man's face.

"That's it. That's enough," the man said menacingly, and Paul watched him reach for the gun in his pants. I'm dead, Paul thought. But I was dead anyway, there is no escaping this. The man took the butt of the gun and hit Paul in the temple. Paul went down and floated up again. Another eternity went by before light came into his vision and he realized where he was. He was on his knees, an unbearable intense throbbing in his head. He was eye level with the man's crotch. With nothing left to lose, Paul headbutted the man in the groin. He heard the man say "oof" and saw the gun drop with a dead and impotent thud to the ground. Paul felt a weight as the man doubled over on top of him. With his powerful and freshly shaved legs, Paul lifted and put the man on his shoulders. He felt the man punching, but with determination Paul kept his momentum and threw the man off his back and over the bridge railing behind them. There was a feeling of a weight off his shoulders and the sound of a splash and a crack from the riverbed below. Paul fell back to his knees, confused, and saw the gun laying near him. He reached for it, clutched it in his hands uncertainly, and knew he was not going to die today.

"Jim!" he heard the Latino scream. Paul held the gun and fell to his bottom and crab walked away as far as he could. He sat and tried to clear his vision. His friends were huddled by the cars and the Latino was leaning over the bridge shouting for his partner. "Jim!" Silence. "Jimmy!" The only sound was the wind blowing through the trees, somehow louder now that the sky was going dark. The Latino turned to Paul and pointed at the railing. "Get down there," he shouted. He did not sound Latino, after all, Paul thought. "Get down there and see if he's hurt, you dumb fuck!"

Paul got to his knees and managed to stand. "No," he said. His voice shook in harmony to his legs. He heard a scream and a man's voice shout Marie's name. There was movement in his peripheral, but all he felt was the gun in his hands.

"What the fuck is wrong with you?" The man walked towards him. Lance. His name was Lance, Paul remembered. "We told you we were going to let you go!" Paul raised the gun and aimed at the man. "Whoah, lady," the man said and opened his arms as if for a hug. "Take it easy, now."

Paul held the gun, and his arm shook uncontrollably. "You lied to us. There was no way you were letting us go."

"Hold on, you don't want to do anything stupid."

"Really? Did you think it was stupid for your friend to shoot me?" Paul said. "And your boss took off somewhere to kill Larry. Did you think we wouldn't clue in?"

"My boss?" The man looked around, confused. "What the fuck?" He held one hand out to Paul and with the other reached in his pocket for his phone. "Just wait, lady. Hold on."

"My name is Paul, not lady!" Paul shouted, tears of frustration building in his eyes.

"Let me make a call." The man dialed his phone and after a few seconds, said, "Ron, it's Lance. We got a problem here. Where the hell did you go?" He pressed end, put the phone back in his pocket and held his hands in the air.

"Where did your buddy go?" Bryce suddenly spoke up. "Where did he take Larry?"

"He took him somewhere to shoot him," Paul sobbed and tried to keep the gun steady.

Marie shrieked. "They are going to kill us!"

"No one was going to shoot you, in case you haven't noticed, this lady... sorry, Paul... Paul has the gun," Lance said. "Just, please, let me check on Jim."

"What was the plan, Lance?" Bryce said and took a step forward. "Where did your buddy take Larry?"

"I don't know! Fuck!" Lance shouted.

"You were just going to kill us? Without even thinking?" Bryce asked. "Without even considering our families? How would your wife and kids feel if you died?"

"I don't have a wife and kids," Lance said and pointed at Bryce. "Just stay back."

"Well, your parents, then? How would they..."

"I haven't seen my folks in ten years, if that's any of your business."

"Oh," Bryce said, "well, friends, then?"

"Not really," Lance said. "Ron. And who knows where the hell he is. And Jim. And I would like to see if he is ok. Just back the fuck off and let me check on Jim."

"Go," Paul said, and stepped away from the bridge, the gun still aimed at Lance, more or less. It shook to the sky, to the man's face, to his knees, to his shoulders, to the sky again. Why was it so heavy?

"Paul," Lisa was beside him, a gentle hand on his shoulder. "give me the gun, Paul. Before someone gets hurt. Just let me have it."

Lance walked to the railing and leaned over. "Jim!" He shouted.

"Paul, that gun will go off the way you're holding it. Give it to me." Lisa's voice was so calming and reassuring that Paul stopped shaking. He handed her the gun and sunk to the ground. He held himself around his shoulders and wished, for the first time in his life, that his brother was there to tell him what to do. Should he feel brave for saving his friends from a dangerous man? Should he feel like a hero? He did not. He recalled the feeling of strength he got earlier in the day when he was dressing in his wife's clothing. It felt as though he had accomplished something. Was he brave then? Yes, he felt brave then. He felt he had done something Gordon Zanders had not. He had held that man in his thoughts all these years and had been ultimately disappointed. Gordon Zanders held a secret that he had no reason to. Paul would not be ashamed. This morning, he felt like a man. In a dress. And holding a gun and saving lives did not even come close to that earlier feeling of empowerment.

"Jim!" Lance screamed again. He pulled his phone from his pocket and used the flashlight over the edge of the bridge. Paul watched Lance focus on something in the dark below and saw his chest heave. He spun around and glared at Paul. "He's dead, you fuck!" he shouted. "I am going to fuck your shit up." Paul heard screams as Lance charged towards him. Paul covered his eyes, waiting resolutely to have his shit fucked up.

Lisa pointed the gun steadily at Lance and shot him between the eyes. A red dot formed in his wrinkled brow and began flowing blood. Lance's eyes widened and he dropped to his knees. It seemed to Paul that even the wind stopped blowing as Lance fell on his face, his feet still up in the air before finally dropping. There was one shudder and then stillness. Paul crawled over to the man and threw up over his back.

Chapter 18: Lisa

Lisa knew from the moment she watched the big man fall over the edge of the bridge they were in trouble; the plan had changed. She made the deal with Ron and she did not believe he intended to hurt any of them, but the big man with the gun was a different story. There was something in his eyes. Or rather, a lack of something. She had seen that lack in men of his age before, it meant he was done. Done caring about anyone and anything, a man with nothing to lose. When he started beating on Paul, she debated taking the other car and escaping while everyone was panicked and occupied. Something made her stay, though. Why? Was it small, weak Paul? She did feel a little sorry for him, lying prone and taking a beating in a dress. It seemed so pathetic. Then the situation turned, and Paul had shouldered the big man right off the side of the bridge, and that was a long way down. There was no coming back from that.

With Paul waving that gun around, she knew something bad would happen. Was the safety even off? Did Paul know enough about guns to turn the safety off? She went to him and was gentle, but knew she had to be quick. That other dimwit was looking over the railing and, in a few seconds, would find out what Lisa already knew. His friend was dead. She pulled the gun from Paul and flicked the safety off.

Sure enough, the man Ron had called Lance turned and Lisa saw the rage in his eyes. He was coming straight for Paul. Even though he was outnumbered, there would not be anyone to challenge him, as far as Lisa could see.

Marie would be useless, Paul was finished, and that wimp Bryce did not seem to be doing anything. It would be up to Lisa, as usual, to save their asses. So, she raised the gun and shot him right between the eyes, shocked at how quickly it happened. A red dot appeared on his forehead and a small trace of blood ran down his face before he dropped to his knees and finally fell face down on the road, his feet sticking comically straight up before falling too. And then quiet. "Oh, shit." Lisa whispered and lowered the gun. Her knees went to jelly, and she sunk to the ground, placing the gun beside her. "Oh, shit." She whispered again.

Marie was screaming and would not shut up. Bryce grabbed her and held her, but she did not respond, her arms hung limply at her side while she screamed. Paul was sobbing with his face on the ground. "Ok," Lisa said, louder. "We're safe now." She stood and went to Marie, pulling her away from Bryce's embrace, and slapped her hard across the face. Both women were shocked by this, but the screaming stopped. "I said we are safe now," Lisa said to her.

Marie took a few deep breaths and paced around the car. "Where the hell is Larry?"

"I don't know. That other guy must have taken him somewhere else," Lisa said.

"They were really going to kill us!" Bryce shouted.

"I think they would have, yes," Lisa said.

"We have to find Larry," Marie fumed. "So I can kill him before that bastard does."

"We're not going anywhere," Lisa said. "We are calling the police."

"That other guy took our phones. That Ron guy," Bryce said.

"So, we walk?" Marie asked meekly.

"No, this guy has a phone," Lisa said. They all looked at the dead man lying face down on the road. There was an unmistakable rectangular bulge in his back pocket.

"Oh, no. Good grief, no," Bryce said.

"This is not a big deal," Lisa said, and reached into the dead man's back pocket. His butt jiggled around a bit as she pulled and maneuvered the phone out. Paul threw up again. She pressed the home button on the phone until emergency services came on the screen. She pressed 911. In a few seconds she was speaking with an operator. "My name is Lisa King, my husband is Mayor King. I've just shot a man and I think a second man is dead." She explained the situation and assured the operator they were all safe. After a bit of back and forth she lowered the phone and spoke to Bryce. "You better check and make sure that big man is dead down there."

"Fuck that," Bryce said.

"Bryce, what if he's alive?" Marie implored. "He could be running away, right now. Or maybe he is going to come for us again."

"Go, Bryce," Lisa said, and watched him walk unsteadily down the steep embankment until he had to rest on his bottom and use his hands to slide himself down to the riverbed. A minute later Lisa heard a shout, followed by retching noises. "Yes, he's dead," Lisa said into the phone. "Thank you, please hurry."

Bryce climbed back up the embankment and leaned against the bridge railing. "That was gross," he murmured. "His head was all smashed in."

Paul managed to stand and remove his one remaining heel. "Oh, Lisa," he sobbed.

Marie opened the passenger side of her car and sat sideways with her feet touching the ground. Her makeup left dark streaks down her face. "Where do you think he took Larry?"

Lisa knew. Or at least she had an idea. Ron was a smart man, and he had an exit strategy. He was probably headed to the airport and might be there already. But why take Larry? As insurance? That did not sound right, he would not take Larry to a public place, it would be too risky. Leaving him here with them would have been the best option. Lisa did not think he would kill Larry, that was not his intention. He knew he was in deep water and had decided to get out of the pool. Just like Larry had. Or just like Larry had, again. That dirty bugger, Lisa thought, he's slipped off again, clever boy. Lisa had to turn away from the group to hide her smile.

"Marie," Lisa heard Bryce say firmly, "I want you to know that whatever happens now, I am here for you, and I love you."

There was a pause, and then Marie said, "You're an idiot."

In the dimming light Lisa could see the flashing lights of the emergency vehicles from a way off. A fire truck, two ambulances, and four police cruisers, one of them unmarked. Lisa recognized the detectives as they pulled up. The four of them stood helplessly by Marie's car and assured the first responders they were unharmed. They attended to Bryce's nose and gave Paul a blanket. He shivered uncontrollably under it. Lisa told them where to find the second body. The emergency crews went to work, some to retrieve the man below the bridge, some taking pictures, some placing markers in various spots on the ground. The two detectives walked over to them.

"Not a very good evening, is it?" the good-looking one said. Lisa could not remember his name. "Detective Coxcomb," he said and pointed to his shorter partner. "Detective Thorpe."

"That's one way to put it," Lisa said. She did not like the way they were looking at the four of them. Were they not just the victims of a terrible crime? Why the mistrust? They had nothing to hide. Well, next to nothing.

"You know we have a shit ton of questions," Thorpe said to the group. They all nodded.

"I know you all have been through a lot, but we are going to need you to come down to the station," Coxcomb said. "We will have the cars towed in, and we want to have a peek through them, if you don't mind."

"We know," Lisa said.

"Can I call my wife?" Paul said meekly as they walked back to two separate patrol cars.

"You can call anyone you like," Thorpe said over his shoulder. "No one is under arrest. Yet," he snickered. That little pecker head, Lisa thought. She could text her husband on the dead man's phone telling him to meet her at the station, but she did not memorize phone numbers the way she had when she was younger, everyone was in her contacts. She was sure he had been informed already; it was not everyday the mayor's wife calls 911 and claims she just killed a man. He would know soon enough.

She and Paul rode together, and Lisa snuck him the dead man's phone to call his wife. She heard him tell her that something bad had happened, but he was safe and would be home soon. He said he could not go into details right now, but then began to go into details. "Oh, and one more thing," he said, "I am wearing one of your dresses. I'll explain later." Paul had a lot of explaining to do tonight, Lisa thought and smiled to herself again. This was a mistake. Coxcomb caught her expression in the rear-view mirror and was frowning.

Thorpe keyed the radio. "Thorpe and Coxcomb arriving in twenty minutes. Four interview rooms, please. Lots of coffee. Maybe some sandwiches?" He turned to Coxcomb. "Any preference?" Coxcomb shook his head. "Just get what you can get. Or pizza. Yes, pizza. You want pizza, Coxie?"

"Sure, Thorpe." Coxcomb sounded annoyed.

"Ok, pizza," Thorpe told the radio. "Two boxes."

They arrived at the police station and were separated. Paul looked frightened and Lisa held him. "Don't worry, you did nothing wrong. Just answer questions and you can be home soon." She gave him a kiss on the cheek. What the hell was getting into her? She had developed a soft spot for this little shithead somehow.

Lisa sat in the interview room and nibbled at her pizza. Surprisingly, she was not hungry, but she downed her coffee. It was nearly half an hour before Detectives Coxcomb and Thorpe came into the room with more coffee and sat across from her. "We spoke with Marie and your boss, Bryce."

"Bryce Springsteen. The boss," Thorpe laughed and looked at Coxcomb. He did not get a smile. "What?"

"Can you just stop?" Coxcomb said.

"What? It's funny."

"The first ten times," Coxcomb said and Thorpe shrugged.

"And Paul?" Lisa interrupted.

"We have some other officers speaking with him," Coxcomb said. "Because Marie and Bryce have the same story, we are assuming Paul will have the same version of events?" Lisa nodded. "Fine. We believe that's the way things happened."

"Thank you." Lisa started to get up out of her seat, but Coxcomb motioned for her to sit. "More?" She asked.

"Just a bit more," Coxcomb said. "There is something we did not tell the others." He leaned forward and looked Lisa in the eyes. She stared back, not intimidated. "Larry Hansen has been shot. He is dead."

"Larry?" Lisa frowned. This did not make sense; Ron would not have killed Larry.

"Not your Larry from work," Thorpe said. "The other Larry. The one that was missing. One of the Larry's that was missing. Not the missing Larry that you know. The other one."

"I don't know any other Larry Hansen," Lisa said.

"Well, that's not entirely true, is it?" Coxcomb leaned back in his chair. "You were all at this deceased Larry's house when you were abducted, isn't that right?"

"We found out Larry was there, and we were worried about our friend."

"You found out Larry Hansen was at Larry Hansen's home?" Coxcomb asked, "That seems strange to me. Does that seem strange to you, Thorpe?"

"Very strange."

"Ok, don't go all Columbo on me," Lisa said. "We were kidnapped, and they were going to kill us. We protected ourselves and that's all I know. And that's all I really have to say right now, I'm very tired."

"Humour me. I'm just trying to unpack all of this," Coxcomb said. "Your co-worker, Warren? When was the last time you spoke with him?"

"Warren? I don't speak to him," Lisa said. "I saw him at a business meeting, what, two days ago? Yesterday? I don't even know what day it is."

"Well, here's the thing. Your friend Warren is the one who shot and killed Larry Hansen."

"The other Larry," Thorpe chimed in.

"What? I don't understand," Lisa said.

"We haven't told the others, but Warren is also claiming self defense."

"This doesn't make any sense," Lisa said, her composure slipping.

"No, it doesn't," Coxcomb said. "So, I was hoping you could help us out, here. We think Warren and the men who kidnapped you also took the other Larry Hansen."

"Not your Larry, the other Larry," Thorpe said.

"Thorpe, we've got it," Coxcomb turned to his partner.

"I just want to make sure everyone is clear which Larry we're talking about," Thorpe said.

"But why?" Lisa asked.

"We have a theory," Coxcomb continued. "We think they got the wrong Larry Hansen. We don't know how they got him yet. But we think they were after your friend Larry Hansen, and somehow found the other Larry Hansen. We don't know how they were tipped off that he was arriving on a plane this morning, but you all must have shown up at his house just after we got the call that he had been killed.”

“That’s why you left?” Lisa said, hoping she was not saying too much. “We saw you there.”

“So, you go to the house to confront...”

“To help.”

“...to help your friend. He is staying there assuming this other guy’s identity.”

“We were worried,” Lisa said.

“Sure.” Coxcomb looked at her for a long time. If he is waiting for me to break, he will be waiting a long time, Lisa thought. I am the mayor’s wife. I am used to tension. She smiled. “Something funny?” he asked.

“No,” Lisa said. “I just don’t know what any of this has to do with me. We went to Larry’s place and found our Larry with those criminals. If I’m following you, they knew they had the wrong guy, and came there to get the right guy. They took us to the bridge to kill us.”

“That I believe,” Coxcomb said. “And Warren?”

“If that little shit was involved in some shady business, it has nothing to do with me,” Lisa said. “Or Paul. Or any of us.”

“Maybe with Larry?”

“I don’t know anything about that,” Lisa said.

“Did you have any reason to want to harm Larry?”

Lisa hoped she did not pause too long. “No, of course not.”

“Did the others?”

It was a good thing she was not taking a lie detector test, Lisa thought, the questions were making her pulse quicken. “You would have to ask them, but I don’t think so.”

"It's just weird," Thorpe said, reaching for a slice of pizza. "two Larry Hansen's. One dead. One missing... again."

Coxcomb looked over at his partner, clearly annoyed, "Thank you, detective Thorpe, I was just getting to that."

"What?" Thorpe said with a mouthful of pizza.

Coxcomb turned back to Lisa. She really did not like the way he was looking at her. "When you made the 911 call, you said two men were dead and there were four of you."

"Yes," Lisa said.

"Weren't five of you taken?" He paused, waiting. She did not respond. "Here's what we think," he said, finally. "These men were after Larry. Was Larry in some kind of trouble with them?"

"I told you, I don't know anything about that."

"Fine." Coxcomb held up his hands. "You were all in the wrong place at the wrong time. But the thing is, Larry and one of your kidnappers is unaccounted for. Do you have an explanation for that?"

"How would I know?" She leveled a stare at Coxcomb, waiting to see who would blink first. Thorpe reached for another slice of pizza.

"I think you have an idea what's going on," Coxcomb said to Lisa, but before he could finish there was a loud knock on the interview room door.

The door swung open, and a frightened looking desk clerk stood there, shadowed by a tall man wearing a suit and sunglasses in the dim light, his hair slicked back and a lizard string tie around his thick neck. "I'm sorry, detective," the clerk said.

"Jeffrey!" Lisa shouted, relieved.

"Coxcomb and Thorpe," the imposing man said, entering the room and sneering at the pizza on the table. Thorpe swallowed hard.

"Mr. Dahlms," Coxcomb said but did not stand.

"Is there a reason you are keeping my client here for over an hour after the horrific evening she has just experienced? You are aware that this is the beautiful and distinguished wife or our mayor?"

"Just clearing up a few things," Coxcomb said to the lawyer. Lisa saw him sink almost imperceptibly into his seat, defeated.

"Nothing that couldn't wait until morning?" Dahlms boomed and looked at his watch, "Or even Monday?"

"I suppose not."

"I didn't think so." The massive lawyer held out one arm to Lisa. "Shall we take our leave, my girl?"

"We shall." Lisa could not help but grin. She took his arm and stood.

"I have more questions, Mrs. King," Coxcomb said, and Lisa could tell he was not happy.

"I'm sure you do," Dahlms said and led Lisa out of the interview room, "but those questions will come at our convenience, thank you." He tipped an imaginary hat to the detectives and left Coxcomb and Thorpe sitting impotently in the interview room.

"Can you call a car for my friends, Jeffrey?" Lisa said to the lawyer. "They have had a bad day and I would like them to get home."

"Of course, my sweetness," Dahlms said. "Your husband is very worried about you. He got me out of bed, in fact."

"Very sweet of him," Lisa laughed.

"Listen," Dahlms stopped them in the hall and turned Lisa to face him. "No matter what you are involved in, nothing is going to happen to you, do you understand?" He smiled his reptilian smile. Lisa nodded. Perhaps the shoplifting was not going to be the worst thing to happen to her husband's career. It seemed small in comparison. And now, it seemed too small for Lisa.

The four rode in silence and when the town car stopped at Marie's house, she sat staring at where she and Larry had lived. She turned to Bryce. "Can I stay at your house?" He nodded enthusiastically like a puppy and Lisa rolled her eyes.

Lisa hugged Paul when they dropped him off. "Be brave." she said into his teary eyes. "You are who you are, and you are wonderful just the way you are." She surprised herself by believing her words and getting a little teary, as well.

When Lisa entered her home, her husband held her tight for a long time. She told him she needed a bath and a glass of wine and would tell him all about it later. He poured her both and served her cheese and crackers while she was in the tub. He rubbed her back and washed her hair. She sank down in the bubbles and tried to unravel everything. The only one going to jail would be Warren for whatever he had going on. Marie and Bryce had wanted to see Larry for obvious reasons, they were otherwise clueless. Paul was too innocent and had nothing to do with anything. Lisa would claim that she was just helping her friends find Larry. She had nothing to worry about. Of course, there would be police; after all, she had just shot a man. It would all come out in the wash. Perhaps her as a victim and ultimate hero would do well for her husband's re-election. Mayor's wife defends innocent citizens in a foiled kidnapping drug thingy. Beautiful.

Before bed she checked her email and Messenger. Word traveled fast, and so many people she wanted nothing to do with asked if she was safe, and was there anything they could do. She wrote a response and copied and pasted it to everyone. There was one email from an address that was not in her contacts. She opened it. "Hey you. Larry is fine. He wants to be left alone, but he's safe. As per our agreement: I will send you details when I get settled. The people I deal with still think they are dealing with me, but you are my rep so the hand off should be easy. They trust me and know me. Still in?"

"I am," she replied and hit send. Tomorrow she would buy a different phone for these conversations. She felt her nipples harden and something powerful was happening between her legs. She traced her fingers down the walls of the hallway to the bedroom. When she crawled into bed next to her husband, she gave him the best sex he had ever had in all his sixty-one years of life.

Chapter 19: Sole proprietor of the Dew-Drop Inn

This is the type of guy Barry Johnson was. I mean, is. No one wanted to jump to any unfortunate conclusions, but he has not been to work or in his room for about a week now. Barry Johnson invented his own drinks and gave them crazy names for fun. There was nothing culled from the dusty bartender's manual whose only use was to prop up one leg of an off-kilter table. He would just mix things together and try them out on some of the more good sported regulars. Some of these drinks were decent and became novelty items during a two-for-one Saturday special. Some were terrible and led folks to mistrust his next concoction. But Barry would laugh these off as failed experiments, and the next week there would be something new. Most of our regulars are beer drinkers only, so it was a testament to Barry's great character that they would even try his colourful, made up drinks at all.

It was also a testament to his character and how well liked he had become by the way customers took to his Charades Thursday at the pub. It was a treat to watch Trapper Jim come in from his cabin, unshaven as usual and smelling of campfire smoke, and attempt to give visual clues to "Lucy In the Sky with Diamonds." And Tuff, the old timer who had been a fixture at the bar for ten or more years, who came in for three beers at five-thirty nearly every night, who sat in a corner and never said anything to anyone, except to order, and always ordered the same dinner. To see Tuff jumping around and clapping his hands when he was on the verge of guessing some Charades clue. And the waitresses and the cooks who began to show up, while not early, at least on time for their shifts. Who would smile a lot more since Barry arrived. I was smiling a lot more, too. Well.

Barry seemed to bring a bright light into the bar, and it was needed. Winters in the Yukon were cold and perpetually dark. The mood in the bar, and really the whole town, would be solemn for six months until the sun started shining again and the snow would melt and recede, and folks would feel like they were escaping from a dark cave. When Barry started doing dishes and tending bar, it felt like spring had come early. The regulars started talking to each other more and some would even flirt with the waitresses who began to flirt back. Tips increased. More locals started turning up during lunch hour and taking their meals here instead of the newer, fancier places that had opened over the years. On Saturday, people would dance, which had not happened in how many years? The DJ equipment had to be dusted off and overhauled. The occasional Saturday, Barry even served as DJ, instinctively knowing what people would dance to. Mostly old country, and tired 70's and 80's top forty. His between song banter and terrible jokes seemed to please everyone, and it felt strange and exciting having to ask folks to leave the bar at closing time, instead of closing early like we used to.

Barry's happiness and contentment spread like a rainbow virus. Every morning, on opening, he would come down from his apartment over the bar and shout to anyone who was at work, "Good morning! I'm home!" He would walk in the kitchen and say to one of the cooks, "You got a little bit of food on your apron, there." The cook would look down and Barry would chuck him under the chin. The cook would laugh at this and fall for it every time, either genuinely, or out of sympathy to humour their new friend. No matter how lame his jokes were, everyone seemed to agree that he was a welcome addition. We were glad he was here.

He showed up out of nowhere four months ago, smiling and joking while asking for a job. He had such a spark about him that, even though I had not needed extra help, a position was created for him. Soon he was bartending, washing dishes, doing light handyman work, and DJing on Saturdays. He even rounded up local musicians and arranged a jam session on Sundays which brought people in on a notoriously slow day. It was something novel for the locals. An escape from their day to day. When it was soon discovered that he was sleeping in the homeless shelter, I hesitantly showed him the room upstairs over the bar. There was only a fridge and a hotplate and a stand-up shower down the hall. An old couch would have to serve as a bed. "It's perfect," Barry beamed.

Only once did we see a crack in Barry's perfectly shined veneer. About a week ago two strangers showed up at the bar with Constable Dave. They did not dress for Yukon weather, so they were not even close to passing as locals. A woman and a man. Barry's face drained of all colour when he saw them. The woman was pretty, and she and the man were holding hands. The man seemed jittery and out of place in a bar like this. He was a city boy and he kept looking around as if any second he was going to be attacked or a bar fight would break out. There has not been a bar fight in here since 1986, and that lasted all of fifteen minutes; the two fighters buying each other drinks afterwards and have been friends since. Despite his nervousness, it looked as though he had seen trouble before, judging from his crooked nose. The woman walked up to Barry and called him by the wrong name. "It's Barry." He corrected her and she smiled. She handed Barry a manila envelope and asked him to sign some papers and told him she was getting married. Her fiancé had not left the entrance and Trapper Jim had cornered Constable Dave, telling him that if someone did not come out and take care of that grizzly, he would do it himself and he did not give two shits about any fine. Constable Dave assured him he would send Fish and Wildlife out this weekend.

"Congratulations," Barry said to the woman, and we all sort of left them alone and tried not to stare. Obviously, they had a history, but it was their business. "Does that man want to talk with me?" Barry indicated Constable Dave and the woman nodded.

"I'm sorry," she said.

Barry came around the counter and started across the bar, but the woman grabbed him and called him the wrong name again. She held him at arms length and looked into his eyes. She started crying and he held her and was whispering something in her ear. He let her go and she turned away from us and wiped her eyes. Barry walked up to the man with the crooked nose and said, "Hello."

"My dear friend," the man said simply and grabbed Barry in a bear hug. A few of the patrons raised from their stools until it was apparent that this man was not going to harm Barry, he was hugging him. The man with the crooked nose was crying, as well. "We both have some huge stories to tell each other, I think. I'm sorry it's like this."

"It's ok, really," Barry said to him. "I am happy for you both, honestly." The woman joined them. "And I'm really happy here." Barry waved his arm around to indicate the bar, the town, and all of us.

"I'm so sorry," the woman said and called him by that name again. The tears resumed, too.

"Do I have to come with you?" Barry said to Constable Dave. Now, Constable Dave is an intuitive man, and he has lived here a long time. He gauged the temperature in the room immediately. He could sense how solemn we all were and, to be honest, he knew and liked Barry as much as we did. They had played pool over beers many times. Dave nodded that, yes, Barry did have to go with him.

Barry turned and said to me. "I'm sorry, I have to go. I will probably miss my shift tomorrow, but I will be back as soon as I can." He said it to me, but I had the feeling he was saying it to all of us.

"It's no problem," I told him. My customers and staff mumbled well wishes as the four of them left. "Everything will work out, Barry," I said to his back.

Then the chattering began. Barry became everything from a drug kingpin to an escaped serial killer. None of our inner circle genuinely believed it, though. Barry was too good, too kind. A few hours later, one of the waitresses who used to date Constable Dave texted him our questions, and we all gathered around the bar when she read the reply. "Dave says it's fraud or stolen identity or something. He's not one hundred percent sure." They arrested him and were going to fly him south. The bail was set at $2000 which was decent; the judge had been to one of Barry's Charade Nights. We started collecting then and there. Twenty of us gave fifty bucks each. Trapper Jim only had twenty to give and we knew that was a lot for him, so in a way he gave the most. I finally stepped up and offered the balance. What else could I do?

Barry came home the next morning, looking like he had not slept. He thanked us all and said he would explain everything, but right then he needed to be alone. We told him we would be there for him, and if he needed anything, just ask. He had tears in eyes as he thanked us again and went up to his room. We worried all that day and into the night. We sent food up to him and the waitress said, "He looks terrible. He just took the food and gave me a hug and said thanks. That was it."

The staff were surprised, but I expected him to be gone in the morning. I hoped not, and I did not talk about it, but I knew it was coming. His room was cleaned out of his belongings and there was $2500 cash laying on his bed with a short note that thanked us for all we had done, and that he loved us. Fittingly, one of the fluorescent tubes above the pool table flickered and burnt out that evening, and the bar was just a little dimmer than it had been.

Constable Dave was pissed off, but he would get over it. He questioned each of us, but we honestly had no idea. And even if we did ... it's hard to say what we would have done. We really liked the guy. After a few weeks there was no news and things went back to the way they were and stories and laughs we shared about Barry became less frequent.

What no one could figure out was, maybe he did not like who he was, and that's fine. But everyone here loved him. We accepted him and he seemed to accept us the way we were. Trapper Jim with his bad temper and smell. The one waitress who could not afford to fix her teeth but could not hide her smile when Barry said, "Good morning, beautiful." The beer reps who used to just drop off supplies without saying a word, but when Barry was around would stay for a bit and have a smoke and tell some dirty jokes. Barry did not have to go, no matter what he had done. If he was running from someone, or even himself, it did not matter. No one here liked where they were, we all thought about escaping, but we settled in. Everyone loved Barry, so why wasn't that enough?

Get more Buddy Roy Baldry in your life.
He has more books! Check out:
https://dimensionfold.com/authors/buddy-roy-baldry/

Stay in the know - join our mailing list.
https://dimensionfold.com/join/

www.ingramcontent.com/pod-product-compliance
Lightning Source LLC
Chambersburg PA
CBHW060541190726
48283CB00003B/823